THE LOVELIEST OF TREES

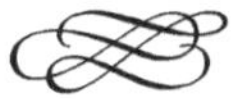

MICHELE DEPPE

The Loveliest of Trees

A Novel by Michele Deppe

DEDICATION

Dedicated to Gwendolyn Bennett and Rick Bloomingdale, for always encouraging me to write.

Loveliest of trees, the cherry now
Is hung with bloom along the bough,
And stands about the woodland ride
Wearing white for Eastertide

From *A Shropshire Lad*, by A.E. Housman, (1859-1936)

CHAPTER 1

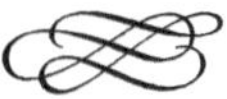

Getting admitted to the clinic had been easy. Getting released was another matter entirely.

It was a worrying dilemma. There had been a lot of discussion in her therapy sessions around having "supportive family and friends." She watched as other peoples' family and friends showed up at the clinic to claim their loved ones and take them home. But she had no one to help her get out of this place. No one to assure her therapists that she'd be well looked after.

If her therapists informed her legal guardians that she was leaving the clinic, escaping them would be nearly impossible.

If she could get out somehow, then she could disappear.

But then something unexpected happened. On the thirteenth day of her admission, she was told she'd been scheduled for a private conference with Dr Crawford.

She'd learnt that Dr Crawford was the senior doctor. He represented the traditional-medicine side of things in this holistic, spa/clinic whose marketing tagline promised "the best of East and West."

But why did Dr Crawford want to speak with her?

She sat on her bed and considered possible reasons, absently twisting her long dark hair into a braid then knotting it at the nape of her neck. Maybe Dr Crawford had received a complaint about her. She had definitely abused the clinic's internet time limit.

Or, perhaps she'd inadvertently broken another of the clinic's rules. The place was beyond confusing. What pleased one therapist was frowned upon by another. They were meant to be offering *integrative* medicine, but the discordant staff was anything but.

She paced the spacious open-plan suite. Could Dr Crawford create certain consequences for non-compliant patients? She said yes to nearly everything offered, from eccentric therapies and intravenous supplements to capsules identified as proprietary blend medicinals. Admittedly, having herself rolled like sushi in detoxifying seaweed had been oddly satisfying. In hindsight, perhaps it wasn't the best course to be so compliant. Ironically, a counselling session this week had revealed that she was generally a doormat sort of person. Hearing *that* had been a bit of a let-down, but (naturally) she hadn't argued.

Whatever the reason for the conference with Dr Crawford, in about two minutes, she'd know. The clinic ran to a perfect schedule.

She climbed from the bed and walked to the window. Below was a lush park, the treetops buffeted by a swirling wind. Beyond, London was sodden with rain. There'd been a feeling of disconnect with the outside world after a fortnight inside the clinic, but of course, that was the point, wasn't it?

It had been difficult to keep her bearings, as she'd spoken only to staff. The clinic was touted as being exclusive, so not the sort of place where you mingled with other patients, referred to as "guests." She had often felt completely alone. Other guests had visitors; their family and friends acted as advocates. Likewise, she'd noticed some guests had personal staff they'd brought with them. She'd learnt from eavesdropping on a pair of nurses ("care attendants") that a pop star was in the suite opposite, to remedy exhaustion and to encourage smoking cessation. The singer's entourage constantly came and went. She saw them bringing through boxes of chocolates, dry-cleaning, and shopping at all hours.

A sharp rap on the door made her start. It was time. She shook her hair loose. Following an inscrutable care attendant down a silent, heavily carpeted corridor; they paused, then were beeped into an office.

Inside, there was a secretary wearing a headset, speaking to someone about guests arriving from Dubai. The care attendant walked past her desk and knocked on a door. Dr Crawford growled permission from within. The attendant opened the door and gestured to a chair upholstered in a vibrant yellow fabric.

The deep, yellow chair seemed to swallow her like a downy canary, leaving her feet dangling above the grey carpet. Her tummy felt nervy. Everything would be ruined if the doctor phoned her guardians to come and retrieve her. From across the doctor's expansive, polished wood desk, which was only a tad less shiny than his bald head, he mumbled, 'Elena Dalca, is it?'

'Yes.'

Dr Crawford read from his computer screen. 'Diagnosis... suffering from stress. You lead a rather extraordinary lifestyle for a young person, travelling abroad and so forth.'

It sounded like an accusation. Elena remained quiet, uncertain how to respond. Compared with the other guests cosseted in the clinic, her lifestyle was the norm.

'Says here you've attended some therapy sessions. Stress management, and healthy relationships.'

She nodded.

Dr Crawford noisily sucked his teeth. He read on. 'Your therapist's notes indicate progress. Feeling much better, I gather?'

Elena wondered if she'd seemed "much better" because she no longer slept in fourteen-hour stretches. She'd been secretly flushing some of the medication prescribed to her; whatever the capsules were, they had massively disagreed with her system.

Dr Crawford typed a few things on his computer whilst puffing out his breath in a ragged whistle. Elena looked about, taking in the tasteful pattern of the carpet, willing the trembling in her body to subside. Emerging from the numbing fog of the capsules had been difficult. Weaning off them caused a strange, random shuddering deep in her ribs. These feverish, seismic sorts of shivers zipped through nervous pathways to her extremities. She clenched her hands into fists to subdue the odd feeling.

A full minute passed. She drew in a deep breath and settled a bit.

Finally, he looked over his half-moon glasses, round nose dipped down, his sagging chins folding together. 'And how would you describe your current disposition?' he asked. His lower lip drooped open as he awaited her reply.

He looked like a toad.

She smiled too widely. 'Quite well.'

He carried on studying her. He seemed to anticipate her saying something more.

Replacing her imprudent smile with what she hoped was a calm, pleasant expression, she declared, 'I feel much more able to cope, now.'

Dr Crawford didn't reply. She clamped her hands over her wrists as a fresh quaking sensation began. Intuitively, she knew she must sit quietly and not panic, despite his interminable scrutiny. He kept on staring and she glanced down.

Muffled traffic noises filtered through the expensive draperies. The shaking was beginning to show, she was sure. Her thoughts grew wilder as the seconds passed.

Stay calm. Perhaps he'd already signed her release form and this was just an odd game of cat and mouse.

Mercifully, he turned back to the computer. She took a deep breath and instantly felt light-headed.

'You'll continue your medicinal preparations, Miss Dalca.'

Definitely not. But she said, 'Yes, of course, doctor.'

He sat for a moment, staring into space. Maybe he was considering the loss of income if she left?

She ventured a question. The only question that mattered. 'So, you'll dismiss me, then?'

His face folded in disapproval. 'You've been free to leave at any time, young lady. At nineteen, you're no longer deemed a minor in the United Kingdom, and I'm certain you are well aware of your rights.'

Actually, she had no conceivable notion of her rights.

But she should've guessed. Roman had told her that once he signed her in, she wouldn't be able to leave until he came for her. Having seen such things in films, stories about women tucked away in asylums to "rest," she had completely believed him. It was only recently, in therapy, she'd found out that her guardian had lied about heaps of things. She just wasn't sure exactly which things.

But what about having a support system? The therapists had banged on about it incessantly. 'You're not going to phone anyone?' she asked, hoping her voice didn't sound as feeble in his ears as it was in her own.

Crawford was too preoccupied (or bored) to acknowledge her question. He sighed and said, 'We have a lot of people arriving.'

She recalled the receptionist on the phone. Guests from Dubai. No doubt they'd purchase more therapies than she.

Dr Crawford shifted in his chair, obviously finding this interview exceedingly dull. 'And you'll present yourself at our Paddington clinic for an appointment. Monday next.'

Absolutely-definitely-not. 'Yes, all right.'

Pursing his lips, he made another noisy gasp—did the man do nothing apart from sound effects?—as he drummed his podgy fingers on the keyboard. A moment later, a small stack of papers came shooting from the printer, smelling like warm ink.

Discharge instructions. Now things would go according to plan. Because she *had* sorted out what she might do once she was discharged—never mind that that could've been days ago.

He handed her the papers, and with magic precision, the care attendant reappeared to escort her back to her suite. A tasteful, navy linen tote marked with the clinic's logo sat on the chaise lounge. Inside the tote, she saw her crumpled jeans, T-shirt, and her old paint-stained trainers. Beneath the clothes were her canvas messenger-style handbag and her small computer.

Shedding the clinic's organically-grown Pima cotton loungewear, she stepped into her jeans. They felt oddly heavy. Elena caught her reflection in the long mirror opposite the bath. Often described by the press as a "waif," she'd nonetheless lost weight. Her pasty complexion was underscored by the dark smudges beneath her eyes. The enormous amounts of sleep during her first week here had obviously not held her through the insomnia of the second.

Dressed, she sat on the bed and gazed through the window at the bleak March sky. The attendant knocked and held open the door for her. Walking on shaky legs down a corridor that resembled the numerous posh hotels she had lived in over the years, she pushed her hair behind one ear and cleared her throat. Leaving this building was bound to be a bit of a shock. She waited silently for the care attendant to swipe her badge, keying the operation of the lift. The preoccupied attendant turned away without a word as Elena stepped in. The heavy lift doors shut with a squidgy-shush and she grew dizzy from the gentle descent. The doors reopened some seconds later, and she stepped into the clinic's stark atrium with a clattering faux waterfall. The receptionist didn't look up as she passed her expansive desk.

Elena pushed through the heavy glass door and found herself encased between high brick walls, with a canopy of frosted glass above. She'd been through paparazzi-free exits before, but never without a car to meet her. Turning down the narrow back street to the way out, she shouldered her way through a heavy metal gate. With mechanical rudeness, the hinges of the gate resisted her push and then savagely clamped shut behind her.

Suddenly, she was on the pavement, standing in a heavy rain shower with people streaming past.

She was chilled. Frightened. And for the first time, free. Joining the flow of pedestrians, she went to the next corner,she crossed the street, then turned south.

ELENA CLUTCHED her arms across her middle as she traversed the streets of London, hopelessly lost. Her phone corrected her misinterpretations of "west" and "south," sending her in circles, which added to her rising sense of panic. Nausea tempted her to hail a taxi and turn for home. Her guardians, Roman and his wife, Nichola, would probably still be away. She could nip unseen into the house and sleep there, just for tonight.

She resisted the temptation. No matter where she was, she wouldn't feel any better, physically, until her body purged the holistic medicines she'd ingested and the therapies she'd undergone. Mentally, peace would only come with carrying out her plan.

Her stomach lurched.

Elena stopped suddenly, causing someone to pummel her back and swear loudly. She veered in front of other people walking towards her, who zigzagged in response. Desperately, she made her way to an iron railing at the edge of the pavement. She grabbed the cold bars and stood absolutely still, eyes closed, attempting to calm her roiling insides.

MEMORIES of the last few days in the clinic spun around in her mind.

'You odd.' The tiny Cantonese woman had wiped her hands on her orange smock, dismissing Elena's weak stomach as an anomaly. Her fierce brow had twitched over her hooded eyes. 'Udder people has no problems wif my leung cha. Herbs good.'

The herbalist had come twice daily to Elena's luxury suite at the clinic. It was impossible to guess the woman's age; her skin was smooth and clear. The woman stood at her wheeled cart, silently selecting herbs from cotton bags that she drew closed with strings. Expensive bottled water from France boiled in an electric kettle in the suite's small kitchen. Elena had sat at the large dining table, watching. The herbalist pinched the herbs deftly with her fingers and efficiently dropped them into the teapot. When the kettle clicked, she flipped the lid open, allowing steam to trail around the modern glass light fixture. Steeped, the herbal mixture was poured into a smooth brown ceramic cup and handed to Elena. Without fail, the woman then crossed her wrists, tilted her head to one side, and waited until Elena had drunk the contents to the last, eliminating any chance of pouring the concoction down the drain.

At the beginning of Elena's second week at the clinic, she'd been poorly. Her stomach had cramped and a rosy rash had spread across her neck. She couldn't tolerate the dreaded sharp smell of ground roots and herbs or continue to drink what her therapist had called the "cleansing adaptogen preparation."

On Thursday, as usual, the herbalist had bustled into the suite, pulling her cart alongside her.

Elena uttered a child-like refusal. 'No.'

The woman had looked at her blankly. Elena had been frightened, wondering what the woman would do. A few moments had passed, then the herbalist quickly removed her cart and was gone. Elena had relished the gratifying feeling of standing up for herself.

ELENA RELEASED her grip from the railing. Taking a deep breath, she stepped back into the flow of pedestrians. Her mouth felt full of cotton wool. Rest and a drink of water would come later. She must keep pressing towards the station. There was no guarantee that Roman and Nichola were still on holiday; someone may have already alerted them that she had left the clinic. Should they catch her up, they may be able to force her to go home. As weak as she felt, she must carry on.

Today was the day of her escape.

CHAPTER 2

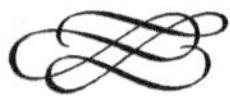

Standing outside the bus station, the lightheaded feeling returned.

Clutching her ticket, she located the correct coach and stepped up to board. By the time she reached the top rubberised stair, there was a burning sensation spreading in her brain. Her vision darkened.

'Hello, love. Find a seat, won't you, dear?'

Elena took a deep breath, bringing the kindly bus driver back into focus. He wore a light blue shirt and a questioning expression. No doubt he suspected the worst, thinking she had a drugs problem. She imagined he'd been a bus driver for a very long time. His tidily trimmed hair and pressed shirt suggested a loving wife. They'd have children of course, and a happy home.

With a feeble smile, she clutched the handrail, took a few steps, and slid into the third seat behind the driver, preferring to stay close. She hoped that he'd maybe glance her way during the trip and decide that she wasn't a bad sort after all. He may even say something kind. Then she'd know he'd changed his mind about what sort of person she was.

Other passengers filed onto the bus. No kids, unless you

counted a pair of teenagers, maybe two or three years younger than herself. A lady with a great deal of shopping came heaving onto the bus and plonked herself onto the seat opposite. The lady then went through her bags, adding small carrier bags to the larger ones, reallocating them to make it all more manageable. A man Elena guessed to be in his thirties sat in front of Shopping Lady. His computer carryall lay on his lap as he looked out the window listlessly. The clouds parted, and the sun momentarily enveloped him in golden light, one of those ordinary moments in life that are glazed in otherworldly beauty. Then the coach doors closed and the engine exhaled a great gasp as the bus rolled away from the loading kerb. Within minutes, they were caught in the surge of commuter traffic.

ELENA TOOK a sip from the bottled water she'd got at the station. Discreetly turning around in her seat, she saw other passengers looking at their phones, chatting to companions, and eating snacks. She leaned her head against the headrest and absorbed the comforting undercurrent of routine and normalcy.

Suddenly, she felt excited. Escaping her life in London was exhilarating. Things really could be different.

She'd begun thinking about leaving her guardians a few months ago, as a sort of New Year's resolution. January's efforts included seeing a solicitor in London about accessing the funds that had piled up in her trust over the years. Then life had got in the way, and she'd sunk into an ordinary work schedule, painting long hours each week.

JUST OVER TWO WEEKS AGO, Roman had swaggered into her studio just as she was prepping a new canvas.

'We're going to accept a number of invitations on the Continent.' Without pausing for a response to his announcement, he'd turned to leave.

In one mad moment, she'd taken action. Before his announcement regarding the tour, she would have carried on procrastinating. She would've stayed in her beloved garage studio at Roman's house, painting her way through another decade.

She squeaked her refusal. 'I can't go.'

Roman stopped. Turned. 'What was that?'

She was humiliated by the huge tears pooling in her eyes. Defiantly, she hadn't wiped them away. This time, she would be seen, if not heard.

Roman had been shockingly diplomatic. He'd smiled stiffly, his voice bemused as he called his wife, Nichola, into the room. 'Maybe the kid has earned a week or three off, Nick. What do you say?' He had laughed then, as though they were all having a great joke.

But Nichola hadn't immediately agreed. She'd taken stock of her manicure, buying time, winding Elena up to the point where she'd forgotten to breathe. But then all at once, Nichola decided the idea suited her.

'It's always about the pair of you--the painter and promoter. Never does it occur to anyone that *I'm* the one in need of a break.'

Elena's tears had streamed then—not from desperation, but relief—as Nichola had smiled and shot up the stairs to pack for "her little holiday in Monte Carlo."

His wife sorted, Roman said, 'I've already worked out just the place to stow you whilst Nichola and I are away.'

'A place?'

Elena had known gaining freedom would be easier if she remained in England. Having a sort of breakdown had bubbled up as an intuitive defence and it had worked a charm. But she'd imagined they'd just ignore her, leave her at home, and she would simply leave.

'Of course,' Roman had said. He'd worn an expression of mock concern. 'You're obviously upset, Elena, and we can't just leave you on your own, can we? You need proper care.'

Her mouth had gone dry and so had her tears. Whatever he had in mind, at least she hadn't consented to be taken on tour from country to continent for the next six months. True to his word, a taxi had come to collect her the next morning. Roman had advised her to take along her handbag, devices, and a few pairs of underwear. Nothing else. Not even a change of clothes. She was going, he'd said, to a very swish place to rest; she ought not to be concerned with the absurd expense, because the benefits would be seen in her work when she returned. It hadn't occurred to her to object.

Later, in the clinic, she'd reflected on this last conversation with Roman and Nichola. Releasing those hot tears had been remarkably easy. Simultaneously, came a realisation that years of suppressed feelings were buried beneath her everyday awareness.

If she were honest, her plea of needing a deep rest--with the added bonus of some counselling--hadn't been entirely unjustified.

ELENA AWOKE to her body pitching forward as the bus came slamming to a halt. Passengers voiced a collective "ooooh," as the coach shimmied and the brakes whined. Outside, she could see other vehicles grinding to a stop; perhaps it was traffic volume or an accident ahead. Against reason, she wondered if somehow Roman and Nichola had learnt of her leaving hospital, and the police were about to board the bus and demand that she return to London.

She had been quite young when she uncovered the truth of her situation. Her earliest memories were of being at a sort of boarding school and wondering where her family was. Then she was brought, aged seven, to England. She was sent to another boarding school for a time. Elena had been happy to assume that Roman and Nichola loved her. She thought she'd been adopted.

She learnt the truth on her ninth birthday. A lot of grown-ups came to an evening party in their palatial house. There was a massive birthday cake, and people took her picture when she blew out the candles. But there were no other children. And no one served the cake. There were grown-up drinks in sparkling glasses. Loud music played. Some people stood laughing in groups on the stone patio alongside the shimmering outdoor pool, where white spring flowers floated on top of the water. Elena wandered about, lurking in corners, listening to conversations, watching and unobserved.

Nichola, whom she'd never been allowed to call mum, was talking with a lady in a shiny silver dress. The lady's hair was silver, too, and Elena wondered if she was someone's granny. The music was louder inside the house, and Nichola was practically shouting.

'A prodigy, that's what the finder told us.' Nichola's white-blonde hair was swept up on her head, her lipstick the same claret red as her dress. She looked like a firework; gesturing, squealing, and ready to explode.

'Oh, is that right?' the silver lady replied.

'Yeah.' Nichola's voice sounded funny, as though she had a mouthful of food. 'But you know, Aggie, that it was my idea, of course. There'd been something on telly, about a kid in America delivering her painting to the president! A child, adding her artwork to what were up on the walls at the White House.' Elena crept closer, hiding behind a potted palm as Nichola continued. 'I told my Roman, I said, that's for us, darling.' What with all those stupid paintings fetching thousands of pounds!'

The silver lady laughed with Nichola. 'How'd you know, though, that Leanna could do it?'

'"Eee-lane-ah,"' Nichola corrected. This made them laugh, too. 'Elena's parents had been artists in some odd little country called Moldova. They both died. So, we found this little girl, didn't we? Sent the Wolf, an old woman Roman knew was right for the job, to pick a prodigy out of an orphanage.'

'And Elena was painting already, at that young age?'

Nichola drank to the bottom of her wine glass. 'No, no. Never let it be said that Roman doesn't know how to take a risk! No, she didn't paint. But she was drawing, waaaayy beyond her age.' Nichola burped. 'So we just kept her on her own, you know —no distractions, like. That child's always had the very best art supplies, I can tell you. In no time at all, lo and behold'—Nichola batted the silver lady's arm—'she painted up a storm. Elena's the darling of the art world, you know; our little goose that lays the golden eggs. Of course, she'd be nothing without Roman; he's always putting her in front. He's the best promoter in the UK. He could make the Eskimos believe they need…ice, is it?' Nichola swayed and her words sounded funny. 'What I'm saying there, Aggie: Roman always gets what he wants. My charmer, that's what he is.'

'Oh, yes, quite.' The silver lady yawned and then waved her hand. 'And she's a pretty little thing. But what happens later, if she starts being troublesome? Moods and boys. Not too many years distant, is it?'

In the shadows, Elena froze, listening for Nichola's answer.

'Why, she'll be out on her ear, the very moment she's ungrateful!' Nichola's face screwed up in a deep scowl, as though Elena had already been very bad. 'Believe me when I say it's all legal on our side.' Nichola looked at her empty wine glass and frowned. 'Oh…'

'You've protected yourself,' said the silver lady. Nichola stared at her. 'You said it's all legal, with the little girl.'

'Ah, yesss. A nice bit of the dosh goes in a trust for her, but we've no further obligee—ob-li-gay-shuns. It'll be back to an orphanage if she starts getting above herself. And if I found one little artist, there's always another, am I right?'

Holding her hand over her mouth, Elena slipped away from the birthday party. Roman found her later, still in her best dress, furiously painting in the garage of the grand house. She'd been working from a sketch of a little girl that was in her mind. A girl who'd been her best friend. A girl that--she now understood--had been a fellow orphan.

THE BUS BEGAN MOVING AGAIN. Elena sighed. The euphoria of freedom had gone. But at least she was no longer under the tyranny of her guardians, or in the strange environment of the clinic.

Left alone to paint what she liked, safe in her own company.

That, she thought, *is going to be brilliant.*

WHILST AT THE CLINIC, Elena had used her limited computer privileges wisely. She'd purchased a new phone with a fresh number, although she kept her old email address. Then she'd opened new accounts and transferred some funds. The preliminary meeting with her solicitor weeks ago was now invaluable; he'd sent over documents to sign and carried out several duties they'd discussed–namely, securing a place to live, where she wouldn't risk ever running into Roman, Nichola, or people from London. It all had seemed easy. And impersonal, as though she was playing admin assistant to someone else. Her level of thorough planning was surprising and secretly made her feel proud. She'd even thought to pay Nichola's housekeeper's daughter, Regina, to pack her few personal items in storage.

Based on their mutual dislike of Elena's guardians, Regina could be trusted.

Elena had travelled the world, but she'd never been to the West Midlands. A website described Shropshire as a beautiful, quiet, unspoilt part of England. And so, she'd searched online for a beautiful, quiet, unspoilt part of it to call her own.

She'd had a single requirement for the estate agent: her new home must have a studio with excellent lighting. A nice-sized space where she could paint without interruption.

Running a bit late, the coach rolled into the county of Shropshire over three hours later. Still about an hour's drive from the final destination of her own property, she was at least safely away from London, and that would do for now. She could afford to rest. Tardiness no longer mattered. Gone were the days of chaotic schedules, press interviews, and being taken by drivers to soulless hotels. Instead, she hired a taxi and booked into a cosy 17th-century inn close to a town called Telford.

Elena Dalca was a huge step closer to beginning a new life. But how far behind would Roman be?

CHAPTER 3

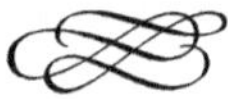

Twenty-four hours had passed since she'd slipped away from London. No one had come after her.

Prior to leaving London, in January's meeting with her solicitor, she had gotten help to take two massive steps: firstly, she purchased a property.

Secondly, she had drafted a letter which explained her desire to live an independent life. The letter was an unusual sort of communication; terribly personal, but printed on Mr DeBoer's officious-looking stationery and bearing her signature in a big, loopy hand at the bottom. Copies of the letter were left on file. Upon her request, several key people would receive the letter through secure mail. It seemed like the best thing to do; the last thing she wanted was people reporting her missing.

During the crafting of the letter, the solicitor's stern assistant had lifted her eyebrow, indicating she thought the letter's contents were a bit soft and silly. She was probably right.

Elena's sense of fairness begged the question: What would her life have been like had she remained in the orphanage? Not only were sour grapes inappropriate in light of all of her blessings, but a letter stating her hurts would have little or no effect as Nichola and Roman were largely lacking a conscience anyway. Thus, her missive was peppered with assurances that she was quite well, quite safe, and thank you for everything they'd done for her for the last fourteen years...but they should not expect to have any contact with her again.

Ever.

Because--she didn't put this part in the letter, either--she'd no longer allow them to control her life and make her miserable.

She'd told her solicitor this. He'd glanced at his watch. She'd stopped talking.

ENCOUNTERING a chatty fellow guest at the inn over breakfast made her realise that to disappear successfully, she'd need to be less than honest. People probably didn't care about who she was, but perhaps someone may recognise her from the television shows and interviews Roman had made her do. Best not, in future, to use her real name or apply for loans.

Whilst away at school--she'd been sent away whilst Nichola and Roman sorted out their marital problems--Elena had completed mandatory driving courses. She'd managed to get her licence but hadn't driven since. Chauffeured cars were always waiting. Now, she would definitely need to drive.

There was a car dealership in Telford within walking distance of her lodging. Along the way, she popped into a branch of her bank in London. She had phoned ahead to give the pertinent information necessary to the bank's manager, along with the name and number of Mr De Boer—in case they needed persuasion from a real adult. Then she waited until the following day to revisit the bank to retrieve payment for a car.

Her handbag contained a receipt and cash. Lots of it.

She carried on to the dealership, walking quickly and holding her bag close to her body.

Initially, she shopped for vehicles best described as nondescript. A rather handsome lad and his sales pitch changed all of that.

'Here's a beauty,' he said. 'Perfect for you.'

He showed her a snappy-looking utility vehicle with loads of boot space, as shiny and blue as a tube of lapis lazuli paint. It was a Citroen.

Elena giggled aloud when she read the name of the model: "Picasso."

Sold.

Rolling gently down the road, she thanked God that her reintroduction to driving was far from London's brutal traffic.

ELENA WAS TERRIFIED to drive any distance, but needs must. She set out very early in the morning to encounter as little traffic as possible.

Her new car brought her to an estate agent's office in the wilds of Shropshire. She introduced herself with a fake name.

The estate agent was surprisingly young, perhaps only three or four years older than herself. He wore a shiny khaki shirt and a cheap tie made of a repulsive brown material. An angry red rash of spots gathered around his chin.

She thought he was rather a nice person.

They sat alone in a depressing office the colour of porridge. His father, he'd explained to her almost immediately, was at a property auction this morning. And he, Bryan Barker, had been trusted to answer her questions, to show her to the newly purchased property in one of the area's smallest villages, and to transfer the keys.

'All on your own, then?' he enquired.

'Just for a time.' She hoped vague answers would put him off.

'All right, Miss––'

'Button.' Her heart galloped with the lie. 'Tansy Button.'

The name had come to her yesterday when she'd been lost and come upon a garden centre. She'd lingered about, looking at this and that. From a seed packet, she'd read "Common Tansy." Printed below was another moniker for the humble, sunshine-coloured flowers: "Golden Buttons." She'd turned over the packet. *This pungent perennial was once important medicinally, but is now seldom-used.*

That suits, she'd thought. She desperately wanted to be a common person. And she wished to be no longer used.

'Miss Button,' the estate agent repeated. He assumed an important air. He was intent on being quite professional and thorough so that he could tell his father how he'd vetted her, the newcomer to an area where there seldom came anyone new, save the babies born to it. He peered at her and said, 'I was given to understand the owner was collecting the keys. We'd been given an email in case it was needed as a contact. A lady named--'

'Oh, yes, of course. My aunt,' she said, hoping to look genuine, and wanting very badly not to hear her name spoken aloud. 'She'll be joining me later,' she said. She'd work out in the coming weeks how to dispose of the fictitious aunt if Bryan Barker told anyone the story. 'I came along early because there's such a lot to do, isn't there? When one moves house, I mean.'

Naturally, he didn't know what she meant. Not from experience, anyway. Surely, his mother had made his breakfast this morning, as she had done all his life. But far from feeling judgmental about his domestic situation, she envied him. Elena couldn't remember anyone--that is, anyone not employed to do so --making her a home-cooked breakfast, and then sitting down to eat it with her.

Bryan Barker looked at her suspiciously. No, that wasn't fair. It wasn't suspicion, for all of his correctness of procedure. It was simple curiosity. After all, he probably knew something about nearly every family in the area.

But she was a stranger.

She knocked together Tansy Button's history as she went. Hopefully, she'd be able to remember it. 'My aunt isn't very well, you see. I'll need to ready the house for her.'

Her hope that he'd believe the fabrication must've registered on her face as "sincere vulnerability," because he said, 'I'm sorry to hear that, miss. It's a hard thing when someone is just that ill, isn't it? A lot of work for you, I imagine.'

It was good luck that she'd landed on this scenario for her made-up life. She could suddenly see the possibilities.

'Yes, I'm afraid that being homebound is part of the bargain. I don't suppose you'll see much of me, I mean us—in the future. Especially not my aunt…'

'Certainly. The actual owner of the house is a bit of a mystery,' he said, reading from the papers in his hand and smiling at his clever deduction. 'Listed as a privately held company.'

He levelled his eyes at her, waiting for her to supply the company's name. A bit of further proof before he handed over the keys.

'Sacred Studios Unlimited.'

He leaned away from her, considering. 'And your aunt? I'm afraid I didn't catch her name.'

She smiled and added, 'Just Auntie Em.' Oh, dear. Wasn't she from *The Wizard of Oz*? 'She's never called by her proper name. A sort of nickname, I suppose.' It was like she couldn't stop.

An empty silence followed and Elena realised she ought to stop swinging her foot to and fro. If she wasn't particularly skilled at lying, she found it even more difficult to be assertive, but she must try. Setting boundaries right at the beginning would be the best thing. Hopefully, he would take her story to the pub, saving her having to lie on an individual basis to everyone and anyone she happened to encounter.

She hardened her voice. 'My aunt has paid quite a bit of

money for a little peace and quiet, hasn't she? I intend to help her achieve it. For her health.' Unexpectedly feeling the truth of her words, she added, 'Her life has been rather demanding lately, and she's entitled to her privacy.'

Put on the back foot, the estate agent was quick to agree. 'Yes. She ought to have the lifestyle she hoped for in her purchase of the property.'

Then Bryan Barker leaned forward again, obviously not offended.. 'If I'm honest, this has been one of the largest sales, especially of a small holding, that my dad has handled in his career.'

His pride in his father was evident. Ordinarily, his neighbourly warmth would make her smile. Because, ordinarily, she was a friendly person. But she couldn't afford to smile now. The price she'd paid to sneak away, the secret purchase of the house, and her need for solitude were too dear to jeopardise.

He sensed her reticence and blushed.

'I'll just get the keys, shall I?'

CHAPTER 4

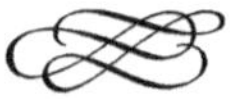

Soon, she would see it in person. The property.

Her new home.

People bought everything online. But perhaps she was the only one to purchase property over the Net. Worse, she hadn't really paid that much attention to the posting.

They walked through a woven steel fence to a cramped car park. This area also served as home base for Bryan Barker's father's other businesses--sales of used farm implements and also of tombstones. Hearing birdsong on the sweet-smelling spring winds helped to calm her. She got in her vehicle, started it, and reversed out into the road. She drove slowly, lagging behind Bryan's small late-model hatchback, still getting accustomed to the new-smelling, bright blue MPV. They passed through the village of Pulverbridge and then left again on the main road towards the village of Marris Mynd.

The surrounding Shropshire countryside was as beautiful as the description in the article she'd read. The green velvet hills gently rolled towards taller elevations with tan craggy peaks.

About six minutes later, Elena followed Bryan into the village she'd call home.

'All right, Tansy Button,' she murmured to herself. 'Thus begins your new life.' A smile cupped her cheeks.

She hadn't supposed that she cared about the village, but now she realised it mattered a great deal. Following her estate agent's car around the bend brought them right into the heart of the village. Her breath caught in excitement. It was idyllic.

The first building she saw upon entering the village was a grand black and white Tudor, surrounded by an equally captivating garden. Even on a dreary March day, the garden was inviting with its massive stone fountain and large, arching trees. There was a small sign outside the chocolate-box building which read "Marris Mynd Library." She relished the thought of returning soon to linger amongst the books and wander around the garden.

Opposite the library was a stone wall that partially hid a churchyard. She slowed the car. The wall ended and Holy Trinity came into view. It, too, was surrounded by a garden with a massive number of shorn rose canes standing in rows. There was a very old house at the edge of the church lawn, probably the vicarage, and there were cheerful lights glowing from the windows, chasing away the gloom of the grey morning.

Marris Mynd's quaint high street was dotted with old stone buildings, one or two that seemed to be standing nearly in the narrow street. A little further down, a long row of shops on the right—tall, imposing, and Victorian—allowed for a broad walk in front of them. Here, she saw a chemist which also offered home items and gifts; a post office; and a yarn and craft shop. At the end of the row, there was a pub with an outdoor eating area consisting of six mossy picnic tables on a stone sweep.

The three or four roads that marked the centre of the small community had quickly passed by, and now the road climbed. She'd read that *mynd* meant mountain. Certainly not the Swiss Alps, but the grade was steep and the engine of her new vehicle took on a labouring sound as it shifted down to clamber up the road.

Bryan Barker had said that her home was not quite three miles from the village.

They were getting quite close now.

A frisson of anticipation made her pulse dance.

THEY CRESTED THE HILL. As Bryan Barker slowed down his vehicle, nervous energy gathered in her belly.

No doubt this would prove to be the most massive mistake of her life. Was she an impulsive person? It dawned on her that it would've been far more sensible to find a studio to let. It really didn't matter much where she actually slept; the work was everything.

It was useless to panic now. If the house didn't suit, it was simply too late.

Bryan Barker's brake lights lit up, and he turned right, between a pair of grey stone posts. One post bore a smooth square engraved with the word "Bytheway." She carefully turned between the posts and drove down the gravel path heavily lined with trees. The trees thinned and the path became a semi-circular drive which edged an overgrown lawn. Bryan came to a stop.

She parked behind him and couldn't bear to look up at the house. The quivery wave of nausea she'd had since weaning from the medicinals at the clinic came at the worst of times. Like now. She took a deep breath, hoping to settle her trembling tummy. Outside, Bryan looked to be thumbing through messages on his phone.

Steeling her courage, she looked at the house through her vehicle window. Several lines of the brief online description of the house popped up from her memory. The words used were "characterful" and "immensely spacious."

Both terms were an understatement. She stepped out and Bryan came to stand beside her.

'Oh, my word.'

'Your aunt didn't tell you much about the property, I gather?'

Tansy Button didn't reply. All had been eclipsed by her need for a spacious workspace. And despite slowly turning in a circle taking in the panoramic view, she couldn't even locate it.

'No. Auntie only promised there'd be a studio.'

He chuckled and walked towards the house. 'You're in for a few surprises, then.'

She stalled. 'The sign on the post. *Bytheway*. Did someone call it that because it's by the road?'

Bryan replied, 'Well, that is what it means. But I think the parish records would show it was the surname of the original family who built the house in 1939. Dad said most of them died during the war. The last people to live here were called Smith. You must have seen their website? They decided to continue in France.'

'Website? Continue what?'

'Their website of your--your aunt's company's--property. The Smith's website link was in the property description.'

'I guess my aunt overlooked that bit.' She'd had so little time to use the computer whilst at the clinic.

'Anyway, the Smiths wanted a different situation. So they listed this property with my dad and relocated to a new bed and breakfast in the Loire Valley. Been two years or more they've been gone. There aren't too many people interested in a place like this, especially with all the work that needs doing. Dad was really chuffed to have your aunt come forward to claim the prize, as it were.'

'Whatever needs doing, I'm sure I can manage. I'm a dab hand with a paintbrush.'

He frowned. 'I'm afraid it's a real job of work. Replacing the roof, upgrading the boilers, and repairing the gutters and downpipes, for a start. Dad came by a copy of the last survey done, I'll pop it to you in the post.'

Perhaps best to push that aside for the moment.

She wandered away from Bryan, unable to resist the view. The house sat upon an open hill. It was misty, but the landscape stretched out to distant hills which looked blue along the horizon, with an apron of dense fog shrouding the trees in the valley below. Above were some inky coloured birds, wheeling in the sky. They soared so incredibly high, looking out of focus now and again when they flew into a tunnel of fog. It was a challenge suitable for Turner, the contemplation of how one would go about effectively painting misty birds so that they looked truly immersed in clouds.

Bryan was talking about holiday lets.

'Sorry?'

'I said, I thought your aunt must've been particularly interested in holiday lets. In addition to the house's five en suite bedrooms having been used as a B&B—*Bytheway Bed and Breakfast,* more specifically—there are those two cottages as well.'

He pointed. She saw a pair of lovely stone cottages with stout chimneys. 'They look older.'

'Quite right. They were built decades before the house.'

Chancing another look, she turned again towards the house. It stood square, colossal, and proud, with large windows. Rendered with a smooth exterior painted in cream, she imagined co-ordinated country decorating inside and massive reception rooms. The house could wait.

'Mr Barker, would you show me the studio, please?'

'Certainly.' They turned their backs to thc looming house, walking in the opposite direction of the small stone cottages. 'The studio's beside the stables.'

Stables? How many buildings are could there? How can I manage all this?

Feeling light-headed, she slowed down. Her blood pressure dropped to her feet.

Memories broke over her head like a chaotic wave; Roman was threatening her when she had been afraid of making a public appearance. She could almost sense Roman standing close, threatening her under his breath. *You'll do as you're told, Elena. These people want to hear about your work. And you'll speak to them, whether you wish to or not.*

Then Roman went silent.

'...Miss Button?'

'Who?' She found herself sitting on the grass.

'You fainted dead away, miss. Shall I get you a glass of water? Or perhaps you need medication of some kind?' Bryan Barker's forehead furrowed in concern. He was leaning over her, his hand resting on her shoulder.

'No, thank you. I just...well, I didn't have a proper breakfast.' She took his hand and stood.

He held her elbow, steadying her. 'Are you quite sure you're all right? I mean...it seemed you didn't recognise your own name.'

Her cheeks flushed. 'I promise, I'm fine.' He dropped her arm and she dusted herself off. 'If you were faced with the news you'd have to clean all of this, wouldn't you be a bit put off?'

He laughed. 'I would. Remind me, I'll give you the card of a good local cleaner. She took care of the guest accommodations in the past.'

Slowly, he led her through an alley of small trees. 'Cherries. They'll be blooming like mad next month.' Crunching over the pea gravel as they walked through the straight, leafy corridor gave her a sense of peace. She felt her strength return. Despite today's episode of weakness, she knew that each day the medicine's power over her system was ebbing away. She and Bryan stepped from under the curative canopy of the trees onto an open lawn.

'And here we are...'

To the left, a small stable made of rustic, dark brown wood soared up into a point, its roof topped by a weathervane. The studio had the same square front and sharp roof, only she could see large windows, and a small stone porch lay across the studio's front. There was room enough for a small table and chairs should she want a place to sit outdoors.

'Could we go inside?'

'Of course.' Bryan stepped onto the patio and reached up to retrieve a key from the top of the double-door frame. 'Only the finest in countryside security,' he joked as he used the key to open the lock. He pushed open both studio doors and stepped aside.

She walked in and was dazzled by the height of the ceiling and the light that poured into the building despite it being a gloomy day. There were blinds that could be drawn when the sun was too strong.

'Someone has painted here before,' she said, feeling as though her intuition could be counted as fact.

'You're right. A landscape artist by the name of Sides, whom I'm told by my grandfather was quite well-known in the forties.'

The studio inspired her. She was glad that she'd purchased some brushes, paint, and canvases to use whilst waiting for her small storage container to arrive in Shropshire.

This studio, this place to create, would help her heal.

'Thank you for showing me the studio. This is a perfect space for me.'

Bryan Barker was uncomfortable with the wave of emotions engulfing his client. To his credit, the young man smiled professionally, and, with an inviting sweep of his hand, said, 'Shall we go see your new home?'

She nodded. Gratitude at having a permanent place to work gave her the bravery to view the enormous house. They walked shoulder to shoulder in silence down the path bordered by neat rows of cherry trees.

For a person who craved privacy, Elena had many places to seek it. She stood alone in her vast white and oak kitchen, which was warm since Bryan Barker kindly lit the burner on the Aga range. Although courteous, he seemed eager to be done with the tumultuous house-showing and key-transfer. She could hardly blame him; who knew when she might fall over or tear up again. After walking through the house with her, he'd said good luck and made his way back down the gravel lane. The silence was deafening.

She'd never been an organised person, and now she hardly knew where to begin. It occurred to her that other people used lists.

So then, for the list: what did she need?

Everything.

Where ought she go to get "everything?"

She hadn't a clue.

Whom could she ask?

No one.

She wandered from room to room. Each of the bedrooms had an en suite, signifying a huge number of toilets to clean, another of the practical tasks that Elena had actually never done. There were other empty rooms besides the reception, kitchen, and dining room, and she wasn't sure what purpose they held. A study? One room had lots of bookshelves and a smart fireplace. A library? Towards the back of the house was a massive utility room and a boot room. She could get a dog and wipe off its muddy paws there. Or perhaps she was a cat person. She wasn't sure. Nichola had frowned on the idea of keeping pets of any description.

An hour slipped away and the gigantic house was rapidly

darkening. An afternoon storm was imminent. She came back to the expansive kitchen and warmed herself by the range. The tour of the house had been daunting, and she felt incredibly stupid. Her thoughts accused her.

The house is more fitting for an entire colony of artists. Not to mention the cottages. I'm on my own in the middle of nowhere. And I've bought canvases instead of having the sense to buy a bed.

Rallying herself, attempting to recapture that intense feeling of gratitude somehow made her feel more ridiculous. And now she truly was hungry. She must work out what to do, as her persistent guardians were no longer here to rule her every moment.

Another stab at a list, then: what did she need most?

Food. Somewhere to sleep.

There was no other option, then, but to get back into her new-smelling car and head back the way she came. She'd seen a few places to eat in Church Stretton, the closest town of any size. Hopefully, they'd also have accommodation for the night. She wearily plucked her keys and her dead phone from the kitchen worktop and closed the door of her new house behind her.

CHAPTER 5

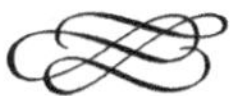

Willa Purslow sat in the kitchen of Myndcroft Hall, an enormous country house that was Oliver's home. When Oliver was home. Which he wasn't, but Willa decided to pop 'round and visit Oliver's mother because she liked her and this morning she happened to be missing her own mum, who lived too far away to just drop-in.

As soon as the housekeeper, Mrs Jenkins, had opened the door, Willa knew something was incredibly wrong. Willa was invited to share a cup of tea. This was monumental, because Mrs Jenkins had previously shunned her, and had managed to do so without Oliver's being aware of her subtle rudeness. But this morning Mrs Jenkins was distressed. Her pettiness was forgotten and she bustled Willa into her kitchen domain.

'It was a most awful row,' Mrs Jenkins said, her expression grave. 'Not in twenty years have I ever heard them shouting like that. Then Lord Ranson came stomping down the stairs, took his keys from the hall table, and we heard his car go speeding down the lane. There'll be no gravel left on it, the way he was drivin' like the devil were behind him.'

'Yesterday?' Willa asked.

'No, pet. That was two days ago,' the housekeeper confided, ringing her hands. 'And not a word from him since. Oh, we know he's more than likely gone down to London. But, well, they've just never had such a row as that. Always ones to sort things out, you know.'

'And Lady Ranson?' Willa asked, referring to Colleen formally, per Mrs Jenkins' preference. It reminded folks that she was employed by esteemed members of the peerage.

'She's not been from her room, not in two days. Barely touched her trays. Never seen anything like it, no, not with her. Not even when she were having a bout of flu.'

Willa stood from the table. 'I'll just pop up and talk to her.'

Mrs Jenkins was on her feet in a flash, catching Willa by the wrist. 'Oh, no, pet. You mustn't. Lady Ranson wouldn't want to see *you.*'

Obediently, Willa sunk back down in her chair.

'I know you mean well, love, but there's not a word you can say as would make a difference, you know,' Mrs Jenkins said gently. 'They've got to mend the rift between 'em. Hopefully sooner rather than later, for their sakes and the family.'

Willa thought it was odd that you could know people whilst you're growing up, but an adult perspective could cast them in a totally different, somewhat disconcerting, light. Willa's earliest memory of her mother's friend and neighbour, Lady Ranson—or "Collie,"as the children called her in those days—was of her stroking Willa's hair. Little Willa held her favourite plush toy, a rabbit called Fluff. The sun was hot on their shoulders. She sat with Collie on a chaise lounge, whose plastic-fabric cushion creaked in a muffled way when they moved about.

'Your mum will be back soon, and we have so much to do!'

'We do?'

Collie made adventures from everything. And she had a little girl of her own, but she was much older than Willa. Older, even, than Willa's sister, Mollie.

'Yes, of course. We'll bring Fluff along to the garden to pick vegetables. And who knows? We may even spot Peter Cottontail or one of his family.'

'Really?' Willa remembered holding Collie's hand and walking across a vast lawn, but could recall nothing else of the garden excursion, or why her mum had left her in Lady Ranson's care in the first place. Had Willa's father passed away at that time? Willa couldn't be sure, and she doubted very much that her mum would remember after so many years. Phoebe, her baby sister, had also been entrusted to Collie's care. Willa remembered Phoebe was in the house, napping, under the watchful eye of the housekeeper. Not Mrs Jenkins; there had been another housekeeper at Myndcroft Hall then.

Willa's eyes fluttered down to her lap. Her engagement ring caught the light and twinkled elegantly. She wondered if Oliver had heard from Colleen since his parents had argued. Oliver was close to his mother. But perhaps not; sometimes parents didn't discuss relationship issues with their children, even if their child was properly grown up and receiving his PhD from Cambridge in a matter of months.

She looked at Mrs Jenkins. 'But surely she'll see me?' Willa questioned. 'Why shouldn't she want to? I'm practically…'

Willa let the phrase hang in the air. Mrs Jenkins looked away. It wasn't that Lord and Lady Ranson had openly rejected Willa, but they hadn't really embraced her, either. It didn't help that Willa's mother wasn't living nearby. Willa had gotten the impression that Oliver's parents hoped he would come to his senses and marry a girl that had "more in common" with the family. Willa was secure in Oliver's feelings. She was proud that she'd recently earned a certificate at the chef's college. Most likely, though, that had only deepened his parents' concerns; Willa had officially become a cook.

Willa was generally mild-mannered, but these suspicions of snobbery made her feel prickly. Colleen had been friends with

Willa's mother, Lisa, for donkey's years. The idea that Willa couldn't go speak to Colleen was ridiculous. She told Mrs Jenkins so.

'Please don't be offended, Mrs Jenkins.' She could see that Mrs Jenkins absolutely was, and there'd be no way around it. Being in the housekeeper's bad books was less a priority. 'There's simply no reason I can't go up and try to speak with her.'

Mrs Jenkins looked rather doubtful.

Willa paused, but didn't answer. She straightened her shoulders. Willa and Oliver's mothers had attended arts council meetings together, shared village life, and stood by one another in difficult times. There was a long history between their families—even their grandparents had been friends, for heaven's sake—and Willa would soon step into the story as Oliver's wife.

She hated asking, but she must; the house was too vast to go wandering around knocking on doors. 'You'll have to tell me, please, which bedroom I'm aiming for.'

Mrs Jenkins sighed. And then, surprisingly, she softened. 'My lady's room is atop the stairs, 'cross the gallery, the first door on the left after you've gone past the hall clock. I wish you luck, pet, I really do. Something's got to be done, and with our Penelope away, and Oliver at uni, well, you're the only one we've got, aren't you?'

Willa stood up again, and Mrs Jenkins joined her.

'Best get my skates on,' Mrs Jenkins murmured.

IT SEEMED to take forever to go anywhere in this house, but this morning Willa was grateful for a few extra moments to think about what she'd say to Lady Ranson of Myndcroft Hall, her future mother-in-law. What could she say? What did she know about complicated responsibilities such as theirs? No matter,

Willa told herself; she wasn't meant to solve any problems, she was here to offer support. That much she could do.

She passed the clock and stood before a white panelled door, edged by moulding and crowned with intricate carving, matching all of the other substantial, ornamented doors in the house.

Willa knocked lightly and called out, 'Colleen?'

Silence. Then the door briskly opened and Colleen was holding out her arms. 'Oh, Willa, so sweet of you to come and look in on me, darling!'

They hugged.

'I've got a nice fire,' Colleen chirped. 'Come in and sit with me.'

Willa followed her into a room lavishly decorated in blue and jade green. Deep carpets muted their footsteps. To the right was a large canopy bed with a white, French-style caned headboard. She joined Oliver's mother in a sitting area by a Victorian-style fireplace with a white marble surround. Willa sunk into a cosy slipper chair as Colleen said, 'Would you care for tea? I'm sure Mrs Jenkins would be delighted for another opportunity to try to feed me something.'

'No, thank you.' Willa hadn't seen Colleen when she wasn't perfectly turned out, looking every inch the country squire's wife. But this morning she wore a pink satin dressing gown, and her blonde hair was caught up in a clip, her face bare of make-up. She was beautiful. Oliver had her eyes, triggering the desperate need to see him. As she did many times in a day, Willa thought *soon,* and focused on the moment at hand.

'How are you, dear?' Colleen asked, sitting primly on her chair with crossed ankles, even here in the privacy of her own bedroom.

'Staying busy.' Willa felt more comfortable updating Colleen on her sister's life, rather than talking about her own. 'Mollie's goat cheese making is going well. Rhys wants to add more acres to the farming operation this year, so he and Mollie have been talking to their customers about what vegetables would be most in demand.'

Colleen asked after Willa's mother and stepfather. 'And how is Lisa? Are she and Sam coping well with being middle-aged parents, do you think?'

'Yes, they love it. Although Mum is really thankful that little Elliot is progressing well with potty training. And my sister, Phoebe, has been a real help with looking after the baby. She wasn't very keen before, but now that Elliot has fewer nappies, she seems to be more willing to take him on.' They shared a laugh, both of them well familiar with fifteen-year-old Phoebe's prima donna tendencies.

But then the moment arrived. Colleen said, 'I suppose Mrs Jenkins has told you that Alex and I had a massive row.'

'Is there anything I can do to help?'

Oliver's mother smoothed her dressing gown. 'No. I'm fine, thank you.'

The fire crackled and filled the quiet between them.

Willa asked, 'I suppose there are a lot of changes he's coping with at the moment?'

'Yes,' Colleen answered with a resentful smile. 'Let's just say England's leaving the European Union has left some out in the cold.'

Willa didn't know much about Lord Ranson's various business interests, but she recalled hearing that he was involved in import/export. 'Is Alex able to anticipate, yet, what damage control will be, following on the new policies?'

'You are very bright, Willa. That's precisely what he's been busy doing. Bailing water out of the boat, so to speak.' Colleen sighed and looked at the fire.

Willa was unsure whether to ask her anything else. Had Oliver's father been in touch? Did she know where he was?

Colleen may not want to tell Willa that she hadn't heard from her husband.

Willa asked, 'How are you coping?'

It was a step too far.

Oliver's mother stared at her a moment. Then she turned to gaze out from her window.

'You're sweet to be concerned, Willa,' Colleen said, nettled. 'I'm sure I don't mean to keep you. You must be so busy, working on the farm, or whatever it is you do.'

Willa's mouth dropped slightly, recognising the cold dismissal for what it was. Quietly, she rose, walked out of Lady Ranson's bedroom, and slowly pulled the door shut behind her.

CHAPTER 6

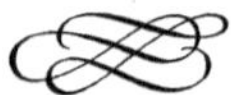

Elena was in awe of the kindness shown to her by strangers. First, Bryan Barker, who'd been supportive during that emotionally wobbly visit to her new property. The kind waitress at the pub in Church Stretton, Alison, who had suggested accommodation, then used her own mobile to ring the bed and breakfast, enquiring as to whether or not there was an available room. There had been. Elena had paid for the room with cash and gratefully climbed the steep stairs to a room at the back. There, with a full tummy, she nestled into soft white linens and fell into a deep sleep.

She only returned to her property to paint during the day. Painting worked its magic for her, providing an unassailable distraction. The studio was a dream come true. Even walking towards it, down the path lined with cherry trees, gave her joy and primed her for work. The studio was a perfect size. The large windows embraced whatever natural light was to be had no matter how grey the skies. In honour of the famous previous artist in residence, she had begun painting a landscape from the window.

In Church Stretton, Elena purchased several items for the

main house: a tea kettle, a mug and tea, a bit of cheese, and a box of biscuits. At lunchtime, she nipped into the house, warmed her fingers, enjoyed a cuppa and a nibble, then it was back to the studio.

At the end of her workday, she had returned to the same gastropub for the same gourmet meal (a nourishing "grass-fed beef lasagne with a radish and celeriac salad," served to her by Alison) after which she slept as peacefully as a newborn.

On the third day, she sat alone in the dining room of the bed and breakfast.

Today, she challenged herself, *will be different.* She would do a bit of exploring at her new property.

Elena drove through a spring shower to Bytheway. The tyres crunched onto the gravel drive and as the house swooped into view, its sheer size intimidated her all over again, with its yawning, empty, cheerless rooms. She parked in front and walked into the house, directly to the room that had served as the Smith's office.

The heavy iron keys to the stone cottages hung from a wall hook. She took their cold weight in her palm, closed the door of the house, and ventured across the lawn.

She came first to the smaller cottage, its door and window frames painted a faded scarlet. Hopefully, no wildlife had taken up residence. She turned a heavy key in the lock. The bulky wooden door creaked as she pushed it open.

The cottage was a surprise, but a most pleasant one.

Beautiful dark beams framed the steep, high ceiling of the open-plan lounge and kitchen. There was a wood-burner set into an old stone fireplace and a pair of bespoke bookshelves on either side. She crossed the lounge, pushed open a door, and found a generously sized bedroom. In the centre of the room stood a black iron bed frame that looked quite old. Coarse, yellowed linen curtains sagged at the window. Another door on the right led to an en-suite bathroom with an old-fashioned bath, full of dust. She left the bedroom and went towards the kitchen. Pine fitted cupboards provided considerable storage. Red, green, and cream tiles covered the wall behind a rustic Belfast sink.

After taking a satisfying look about, she sped over to see the second cottage.

It was much like the first, but the door was the colour of dark evergreens, with matching window trim. The second cottage repeated the open-plan living space, but this cottage boasted a loft, and she scrambled up the narrow stairs to see it. The loft had steeply sloping walls like an attic, a fitted wardrobe, and a view from a large central window that could mesmerise her for hours. Elena came down from the loft and headed towards the bedroom. This bedroom also had an iron bed, finished in grey, with dirty white linen curtains. The bathroom was larger, with a wide basin that had room to set small things around it, and a stainless-steel shower mounted high over the bath. The kitchen was done in green tiles the colour of a sage leaf, with oak fitted cupboards.

This is where she would live.

The cottage suited her down to the ground and was completely to her taste. Elena laughed, because she'd not known what her preferences were until she'd walked through the door.

That evening, back in her room at the B & B, she had a glorious shop online, buying delicious items to fill her stone cottage. Sitting at the small table in her room, she chose pieces of furniture, linens, lamps, and rugs as she ate pieces of spongy chocolate cake she'd brought from the pub.

The online shopping spree was good fun until her mobile shrilled from its place on the nightstand, startling her. The chocolate cake went flying, the icing causing a greasy brown smear on the white duvet.

The mobile rang like a scream. A pause. Then another scream.

She leaned towards it, feeling sick coming up her throat.

An unidentified number.

She'd never spoken to anyone on this mobile.

What if her guardians, Roman and Nichola had managed to discover her number? Was that possible? And if they had deciphered her number, could they also locate her?

The screaming ceased as the call went to voicemail.

She clamoured off the bed. The cake rolled off the duvet and onto the floor, the plate and fork following. Standing in her sock feet next to the cake, she cupped her hands across her nose and smoothed her cheeks. The pressurised anxiety made her feel as though she may burst. She needed to get some air. Stepping quickly into her trainers, she stuffed the mobile into her pocket, grabbed the key to her room, and walked out of the door. Elena took the private stairs at the back of the lodge. Against a tidal pull, she ambled on shaky legs towards a nature path that bordered a small pond.

The night air was wet with mist. Darkness swallowed her, the scant moonlight providing just enough illumination to see. There was a faint splash in the pond and a dog barking in the distance. The path began to bend this way and that, and she tripped on a tree root. Catching herself, she kept moving, breathing, walking out of the overwhelming weight of fear.

The freedom calmed her. She could walk when she wanted, wherever she wanted. There was no one she needed to ask for permission, no travel itineraries, no press interviews. Just putting one foot in front of the other. She could walk all night if she wished.

There was a spot she remembered from walking this way the day before, on the edge of a car park, where there would be lights and a place to rest. She walked on for another fifteen minutes. She arrived at her destination slightly breathless. Sitting down on the bench between the car park and the pond, she drew the mobile from her pocket.

Now she felt able to confront the call.

Pressing it to her ear, Elena held her breath, closed her eyes, and listened to the message.

Elena, said the male caller. She recognised her solicitor's voice. *It's Tobias DeBoer. Apologies for the late hour. I was to ring if there was any reaction to your letter. Well, your ex-manager came by the office, made a bit of a scene.*

Her breath caught in her throat. As she listened, she looked about, as though Roman and his odious wife would suddenly find her sitting by a pond in the dark.

Naturally, I told him you've left no further information. I advised him to leave you alone and reminded him he has no legal rights with regards to pursuing you. I'm available if you have any questions.

She stared at the mobile in her hand, turning the message over in her mind.

Your ex-manager came by the office, made a bit of a scene.

She'd dreaded being pursued and confronted. Her fear had been justified. During her time in the clinic, she'd fantasised that he and Nichola would gratefully acknowledge that they'd had a lovely partnership with her. They'd concede Elena had grown up and needed independence.

But that had been expecting far too much of them. They were angry. The question was, to what lengths would they go to reinstate themselves in her life?

Elena wanted to believe that after arriving home from Mr DeBoer's office, Roman had realised his defeat.

Instinct warned her otherwise. Roman and Nichola wouldn't simply let her go.

She sat for some minutes thinking, until realising she was chilled. Standing up, she felt the beginnings of a headache coming on. Perhaps she would've felt better if she'd tried to wean off the medication more slowly, but there was no backtracking now.

It would make her appear odd, but she was desperate for

warmth, so she walked on towards the village. She re-entered the pub, where she'd eaten dinner three hours earlier.

Alison was clearing a table. 'Can't stay away?'

'Restless,' she answered. Elena walked up to the bar, asked for a drink, and paid with cash. She took her cider to a quiet corner and sat down to sip and consider. Roman had been angry, indifferent to the intimidating presence of her solicitor. She remembered Roman's flashes of temper, the way his face flushed and the veins in his neck sprung into tight cords. His wife, Nichola, was a different kettle of fish altogether. Scheming, plying her victim with guilt, she'd work you like a cat ready to seize a tender mouse. They had manipulated Elena with their alternating fire and ice, one way or another extracting from her exactly what they wanted.

But no longer.

Mr DeBoer had assured her that they had no legal rights to her work or her life. She was nineteen, an adult, as Dr Crawford had said—in fact, her twentieth birthday was in a few weeks. She should be in full command of the fortune that her art had made. And completely in control of her own life.

She thought of her early, temporary guardian, Réka Lupei, whose very name meant "wolf." It was Réka Lupei who had brought her at a very young age from her native Moldova to England. Elena had been only five when the orphanage turned her over to the silent, frightening woman. Another realisation snatched at her: how much had the Wolf paid for her? Surely, that's what had happened. She had been *sold.* Why else would the orphanage release her to an old woman who was intent upon taking her immediately to another country?

The kindly young waitress wandered over to Elena's table.

'You look worried,' Alison said.

'Are you due for a break? Please, have a sit-down.'

The pub was nearly empty and Alison slid into the seat

opposite her. 'I know I scarcely know you, but you seem rather…stressed? Or perhaps even frightened?'

Elena felt the knot within her turn over and tighten. Her thoughts made her sceptical of kindness. 'Oh,' she replied with a smile. 'Just thinking about work too much. I'm meant to be on holiday, but it takes me a few days to unwind.'

Alison didn't return the smile. 'Right. Yes, holidays can be like that. And then real life catches you up when you get back home.'

What home? Elena smiled and said, 'True.'

'What do you do for work, exactly?'

Elena hesitated. An image crossed her mind-- Alison discreetly tucking a wad of Roman's money into her pocket. 'Oh… Actually, I'm in the process of relocating and changing things up.' She pushed aside the full contents of her glass. 'Well, I'm off to the B & B. Good sleep will sort me out.'

Alison shrugged. 'Yeah, all right. Sleep well.'

She scurried towards the door and called a final farewell over her shoulder. Alison replied and then Elena was out in the street, happy for the soft, cold rain and the darkness cloaking her from watching eyes. She blended into the footpath at the end of the road, taking the route back around the pond and tiptoeing quietly into the back door of the inn.

CHAPTER 7

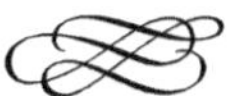

Returning from her late-night hike to the pub, Elena slept soundly through most of the night, then woke abruptly at four in the morning. She lay there in the big downy bed of her rented accommodation, contemplating the message left the previous evening by her solicitor.

Truth be told, she was impressed she'd managed things thus far. She had bided her time at the clinic. Keeping up the facade of mental and emotional exhaustion hadn't been difficult. Roman had always pushed her to do more, especially when art sales were brisk. In some ways, she still felt bone-tired. Somehow she'd endured the prodding therapy sessions (she may've needed a few of those) and the medications, which she felt she hadn't needed, but thought she couldn't refuse.

Regina, the housekeeper's daughter, had often said to her, 'You've got the disease to please.'

She hadn't understood then, but she did now. Regina had been right.

Elena turned over onto her side and gazed out the window. Her view from the bed and breakfast window was a mass of tree branches in silhouette, eerily illuminated by the back door light below. She reached for her mobile from the bedside table. Today's forecast predicted a break in the rain, a cause to rejoice in late March.

She threw back the white duvet and walked in stockinged feet towards the loo, compulsively reviewing what she had done to cut the ties with her old life. She'd ditched her old phone, opened new accounts with a bank in Shropshire, and used an alias to set up a temporary mailing address at a nearby post office.

Had she made any mistakes? Could Roman and Nichola find her?

Four hours later, she'd breakfasted and driven to Bytheway. Today was the best day yet. Though she'd woken up in the wee hours, she woke without a headache. Secondly, a few items that she'd ordered were due to be delivered.

She smiled and turned up the music in her vehicle. It would be a marvellous day.

What she hadn't counted on was having an unexpected visitor.

A SHORT DISTANCE UP the hill from Elena's new home, Willa Purslow sat with her older sister, Mollie, in their farmhouse kitchen. The sisters were enjoying a cup of tea and a slice of cake. Mollie's husband, Rhys Davies, was away delivering some of his fancy veg to chefs who enhanced their dishes with special items grown in Rhys's poly-tunnel gardens.

'Are you finished planting the new field?' Willa asked.

Mollie sighed. 'Yes. But that's not the hard graft.'

'What do you mean?'

'My big-hearted Welshman is determined to turn the farm into a centre of learning. He says Hilltop Farm should be committed to "giving back." We've got our first agricultural students coming this afternoon.'

Willa smiled. She knew that Mollie would be a fast favourite. The students would laugh at her sister's jokes and spoil the goats, and Mollie would love every minute. Far more than Rhys would.

'Any chance they'll help you with the milking?'

'Oh, definitely. Rhys has met with their teachers. The students have to participate and we're meant to fill out slips on each of them.'

Mollie took a sip of tea and turned the conversation on to Willa. 'You seemed upset when you came home from Myndcroft Hall the other day. I saw you from the barn. Did something happen?'

Willa despised putting Oliver's mother in a bad light, but Mollie had known Colleen for decades, too. As a married woman, Mollie would have compassion for Oliver's parents' strife, as well as their financial troubles.

'I think I overstepped the mark with Colleen.' Willa frowned. 'I was at the hall because Mrs Jenkins invited me to tea.'

'Tea with Mrs Jenkins? Did pigs fly overhead? I hadn't noticed.'

Willa smiled. 'Over tea, I had it from Mrs Jenkins that Oliver's parents had a huge row. You know they're not ones to argue, but I guess it turned into a shouting match. Obviously, Mrs Jenkins hadn't seen the like before. I suppose she felt she could confide in me. The argument ended with Oliver's father driving off like a lunatic. Mrs Jenkins said he hadn't been home since.'

'Oh, my,' Mollie said. 'When was this?'

'Three days ago. And Colleen has been keeping to her room. Mrs Jenkins said she wasn't eating.'

'And you thought you'd go knock m'lady into shape, did you?' Mollie laughed.

'Well, what would you have done? She's soon to be my

mother-in-law, so I thought, "sod it, I'm going up there to speak with her." Or listen, rather.'

'I can't believe Mrs Jenkins allowed you.'

Willa blushed. 'She did try to stop me.'

'Was Colleen civil?'

'She was. She invited me into her lovely bedroom. There was a cheerful fire and we sat in front of it and talked. Just chat. Actually, it was she who brought up the row. So, it seemed as though she wanted to talk about things, if you see what I mean.'

Mollie nodded. 'But then it all turned sour?'

'Exactly. I asked her how she was feeling. I knew I probably shouldn't pry, but I only meant it to be an open-ended sort of question.'

'Did she shout at you too?'

'No, no, not at all.' Willa shook her head. 'She made a demeaning remark about not wanting to keep me from my farm work. It was really only a snobbish sort of dismissal. She didn't raise her voice or anything. And you can only imagine everything she's going through.'

'I suppose. When Oliver rang, you told him what happened?'

Willa nodded. 'Unfortunately. Now he's determined to confront her about the way she treated me.'

'Good man.'

Willa objected. 'A bit much, though, isn't it? I mean, yes, Colleen's attitude hurt my feelings in the moment. But, well, surely it's irrelevant.'

Mollie laid a hand on her sister's arm. 'Granny told me, "Your husband needs to show *you* loyalty and love." She said something about it going all the way back to Chaucer's time.'

'Oh, yes of course. Chaucer's *Man of Law's Tale.*'

Laughing, Mollie shook her head. 'How do you know that sort of ancient literary rot? You and Oliver are perfect for one another.'

Willa giggled along with her. 'If I'm honest, I'm glad he's

going to speak to his mother. I don't want to come between him and Colleen. But neither do I want *her* coming between us.'

'Wise woman,' Mollie said. 'Do we have more cake?'

ELENA WAS THRILLED that the mattress she had ordered fitted the old iron bed frame. There was a little gap, but only an inch or so. She'd received an email that one of the lamps would be delayed, and she was looking for the tracking information when a vehicle arrived out front. Probably the delivery of some dishes.

She bounded out of the cottage and into the sunshine, momentarily blinded. Raising her hand to shield her eyes allowed her visitor to step closer without her recognising him.

A moment later, she (literally) couldn't believe her eyes.

'Shropshire? Really, Elena, I thought we'd properly cultured you. You've seen the seven wonders of the world, but the first thing you do is set up house in the nearest cow-pasture.'

Fear knifed into her belly, sending out currents of nausea. Elena had no idea of what to do.

Roman laughed at her, relishing her obvious anxiety.

She had learnt in therapy how to be assertive, but she couldn't remember what she was meant to do. In fact, she could scarcely speak.

'How...'

He laughed. 'How did I find you? You've vastly overestimated yourself. I'll always know where you are, Elena.' His amusement gave way to an intimidating glare. 'Think you're clever, don't you?'

She stood absolutely still. Except for her head, which began to pound so that she felt her body pulsing with reverberation. She mustn't pass out; he had stuffed her, unconscious, in the back of a car once before.

He stepped closer. She smelled alcohol on his breath.

'Don't you think I knew exactly what you would do? All that guff about being exhausted. Yes, I knew you were faking. And all that internet shopping you've been doing...' He chuckled, ridiculing her. 'Silly of you to keep your old email address, wasn't it? Never changing your old password. But then, you were never that bright. A brilliant artist, of course, that's why I kept you for as long as I did, but you're rather stupid, aren't you?'

His eyes glowed with hatred. She'd only ever done whatever he asked, yet he despised her. Elena crossed her arms over her chest as tears spilt down her cheeks.

'What do you want?'

'"What do I want," she asks me. Well, I should think that would be rather obvious. You're due to sign another contract.' He stepped forward and grabbed her by the shoulders. He leaned over and squared his face to hers, eye to bloodshot eye. 'Maybe we can go for lunch. You'd like that, wouldn't you? Surely, they have a pub even this far from civilisation, hmm?' He squeezed the tops of her shoulders until she winced in pain.

Her eyes fell to her feet.

Think, think, think.

She only knew she mustn't get in the car with him.

He unexpectedly let go of one of her shoulders, and she stumbled. Roman turned away. 'Who's this, then?'

She looked up and saw her estate agent.

What's his name?

He'd parked his car in front of the house but was walking towards them.

'Don't tell me you've actually made a little friend. That'd be a first, wouldn't it?' Roman's voice was a hoarse whisper. 'Send him off, or I'll find a way to get rid of him.'

Trembling, she found she could do nothing.

Bryan Barker spoke and Roman ignored his outstretched hand. Upon hearing the young man's name, Roman grinned.

'Ah, our capable estate agent, is it? You've done a brilliant job, helping *us* with our new acquisition.'

'Mostly my dad, but thanks,' Bryan said, obviously complimented. 'It's quite the property. What are your plans for it?'

She could sense Roman's annoyance, but he continued with the charade. 'Nothing very interesting. The space will be handy for family visits.'

Bryan nodded.

'But we're people who keep to ourselves.' Roman's hand moved up from Elena's shoulder to the side of her neck, his fingers pinching a subtle threat. 'I'm sure my niece has told you little about our family. Because we're loners, aren't we, darling?'

Elena swivelled her eyes, daring to glance at Bryan Barker.

Straightening his spine, Bryan's voice took on an unfamiliar tone. 'Well, whether or not that's the case, I'm sure your niece is keen to keep our lunch date.'

Roman's face registered surprise at the young man's boldness. So much so that his grip on her neck increased and she cried out. Bryan immediately stepped forward, forcing Roman to take a step back, losing the balance that was already compromised by drink.

'All right, love?' Bryan slipped his arm around her shoulders as Roman's drew back from her neck.

Then Bryan did something else. He winked at her. Elena smiled, feeling a surge of courage.

'We'd best go,' he said quietly. Elena leaned against Bryan's arm as he escorted her towards his car, leaving Roman standing there, speechless.

CHAPTER 8

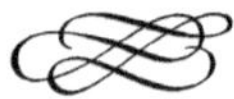

She sat in Bryan's shabby car, trying to process what had just happened. He'd smiled at her, but hadn't said anything since they'd left her former guardian standing in the drive, seething.

Moments later, Roman was following them in his car.

But as Bryan pulled into the pub at Marris Mynd, Roman's vehicle sped by. Roman shot a poisonous look in their direction.

Making eye contact with her ex-manager had made her shudder, but she knew she'd won an important battle—with Bryan's help.

They ordered lunch and sat down at one of the empty tables.

She tried to be upbeat. 'If the food here tastes as good as it smells, then I'll want to come every day.'

Bryan understood her need to make small talk. 'In my experience, Jake doesn't serve anything that's less than delicious. My dad often meets clients here instead of closer to the office just to support the pub. It lets people in on the best kept local secret as well.'

'Speaking of secrets...' Her voice shook with nerves, but she wouldn't repay Bryan's kindness with continuing to lie.

Their food came. Bryan began eating without looking at her.

She cleared her throat.

'My name's not Tansy Button.'

He smiled. 'And here's where I say, "What were you thinking?" Of all the names, that's the most ridiculous, surely.'

Her jaw dropped in surprise. Somehow, she hadn't expected Bryan to be witty. 'I've always known.'

'You're joking. How?'

He finished chewing a mouthful of chips and wiped his fingertips. He looked at her kindly. 'You may think I'm a bit of a country bumpkin. To be fair, I am. But we do have the internet, you know. And I think you're a bit more easily recognised than you suppose.'

'I didn't want to lie, Bryan. I was frightened.'

He laid a hand over hers. 'I know. No worries, all right? Believe it or not, I didn't actually go 'round telling everyone that we have a newcomer called Tansy Button. Or telling anyone that a famous artist had taken up residence. In fact, I didn't even mention you to my dad. Just that the key was safely delivered. So, whatever people think, wherever you've been living and whomever you've said anything to, that's down to you.'

'Thank you.'

'No problem. But somebody may recognise you, as I did. Granted, not everyone pays much attention to the arty types, at least not compared to pop stars, actors, and politicians. Although I can think of one bloke who'd know you straightaway.'

'You can? Who? Why?'

'He's an artist, too.'

Her curiosity flickered. She wondered if this artist was someone that she could talk to about the process, the work of creating. The companionship of other artists was a pleasure she'd missed out on. Roman and Nichola hadn't allowed her to mingle. She was whisked into meet-and-greets to answer questions from journalists, then promptly escorted back to the hotel or studio. The goal was always to keep her working.

'I'd like to explain.' She was impressed by Bryan's integrity. And she was terrified of Roman being at Bytheway the next time she returned. If something happened to her…

'You don't owe me that,' Bryan replied. 'I reckon you have some very good reasons for keeping your identity and whereabouts private.'

She thought about this. It was kind of him and rather special. What did people call it? The expression dawned on her: Bryan "had her back." She couldn't remember someone being loyal to her before without being handsomely paid.

'I do have one question, though,' Bryan said, pushing his plate away. 'What're you going to do about this guy?'

She sighed. 'Honestly, I haven't a clue.'

'Perhaps I ought to put it to you another way. Do you suppose it's a matter for the police?'

Elena stared at him in return. Such a thought hadn't crossed her mind. 'Why?'

Bryan leaned back in his chair and folded his arms across his chest. 'Seems to me that he had his hands on you and that you may find you're a bit bruised by tomorrow. Surely, that can't be allowed to happen again.'

She looked away, feeling wary of him.

'Maybe it's happened often?'

'No.' Her answer was more forceful than she intended. 'Honestly, Bryan, he's never hurt me physically before. He was just *terribly* upset.'

'And that's what I'm driving at. Although it's a relief to hear that you haven't been enduring that sort of treatment, I'd like to be assured he isn't going to return. And be ready for another round.'

'I can't think that he will.'

'How do you know?'

'I don't know! But it isn't your problem.' Her cheeks felt hot. She wished she weren't depending on him to drive her home. How long would the walk be?

'I'm not the bad guy here.'

'Sorry, Bryan,' she said, attempting to sound genuine. She ought to say more. He carried on staring at her, increasing her irritation. 'Would you mind, please, if we just go?'

Without another word, he returned her home. She wasn't sure which was worse: someone abusive who wouldn't release you. Or someone like Bryan, who ought not to care, demanding that you not allow yourself to be hurt.

She found that she was angry with both men. The most appealing thing was to be left entirely alone.

WILLA FILED out of the church with the other parishioners. It was a typically grey March morning. She pulled her coat collar higher against a chilling drizzle that was pattering on the gravel outside the church doors. Two ladies ahead were nattering about knitting projects. Willa was just about to step around them when someone called her name. She turned around.

It was Colleen Corbett. Willa fidgeted. If only she'd left a few seconds earlier, her future mother-in-law would've missed speaking to her.

'I'm so glad I caught you.'

They didn't hug like Willa's family; it was more of a polite press of hand against the shoulder. She wondered if Colleen would ask Willa to call her "mother" when she married Oliver. He usually called her mother, and "mummy" when he was being jokey.

Willa arranged her face into an expression of friendliness. 'Lady Ranson. Quite a filthy day, isn't it? The rain seems to refuse to leave.'

'Yes, but at least it's a bit warmer.'

Willa drew on her gloves, hoping that perhaps this was the end of the conversation. It was cold enough in the old stone church. Her fingernails had a blueish tint.

'Willa, about the other day--'

'No, I shouldn't have pried. I apologise.'

Colleen smiled. It was a sincere smile, not just simply the kind of face one makes when you really do believe the other person is at fault.

'Actually, I mustn't let you get away with that, Willa. Or calling me by a title.' Colleen looked thoughtfully at her. 'I behaved badly, and I must say that I am sorry. My rudeness was most certainly not your fault. Worse, I was being priggish; when the truth is, I spent a lot of time as a child working on my grandmother's farm.'

Willa smiled and looked at her feet. 'Well, it's behind us now.'

Colleen reached out and touched Willa's arm. 'Do come over to the house, won't you? If you don't have lunch plans.'

Willa couldn't hide her surprise. 'I'd love to.'

She got into the creaky old Land Rover that had belonged to her family's farm for ages, and in a few minutes, she drove through the black, scrolled iron gates of Myndcroft Hall. The interior of the vehicle grew darker as the drive was bordered on both sides by heavy woods, then the lane turned to the left and the old vehicle groaned as Willa drove it up the hill. As she approached the massive country house, the trees gave way to parkland. She stopped, parked, and she climbed out to walk across the gravel drive. The formidable front door of the house opened in anticipation of Willa's arrival only moments after Colleen.

But when Willa looked up at the open door of thc house, she was shocked.

'Surprise, sweetie.' In a moment, Oliver was over the threshold and holding her tightly.

'I can't believe you're here!'

They kissed. The rain began to increase, and thunder rumbled in the distance. Oliver grasped her hand as they made for the house. Colleen was standing in the hall, shaking out her wet coat.

As the door closed behind Willa, Oliver turned to his fiancée with a serious expression. 'I felt we needed to sort things out in person.'

Willa's heart sank, wishing the harsh conversation with Colleen could be forgotten. She glanced at Colleen, who mouthed the word "sorry" over Oliver's shoulder.

Willa smiled at her. At that moment, their conspiracy in allowing Oliver to think he was mending things pushed the two women beyond courtesy, and Willa knew that she and Colleen were becoming friends.

IT WAS quiet at the vicarage. More often than not, Veronica would inform him who would be joining them for one of her delicious luncheons after the service. He realised that he didn't know when she made these arrangements, or why she asked the people that she did, but her selections were always perfect.

The vicar looked at his wife now, sitting on her favourite chair. She and her cat were curled up and Veronica was lost in a book. 'You're as beautiful as you are clever.'

She absorbed a few more words and then lifted her eyes slowly, took off her glasses, and smiled at her husband.

'I was just wondering for the thousandth time why you chose me.'

'I adore you.' She stroked her cat as though her heart was full of affection for everyone. 'And you know it, don't you?'

'Yes, I do. I just can't puzzle out why.'

'One of life's mysteries. And probably the fact that no one else would take me on. Would you like some coffee?'

He sighed. 'Just the thing to take the edge off this eternal damp.'

'There's a joke in that somewhere.'

He couldn't see it. 'What?'

She laughed. 'Eternal damnation. Eternal damp. See, you think I'm so clever, but I can't work out how to use it.'

'Ah, yes. Well, maybe no one would think it funny beyond ourselves.'

'Did you see the breakthrough this morning?'

Stephen ought to stir his stumps and get the coffee for them. It occurred to him that his wife waited on him far more than she should. But at the moment she seemed more interested in a chat. It had been a busy week; perhaps that was why she hadn't asked anyone to luncheon today. 'Breakthrough?'

'Yes. Lady Ranson finally fell off her high horse.'

'Veronica...'

'Don't scold me, Stephen. You know it won't improve me.'

'You don't miss a thing, my sweet, that's certain. I suppose if the Lord gave you such a keen gift of observation, I shouldn't complain. After all, it serves me well. You always know whom to ask 'round for a meal and which parishioner needs a care visit.'

'Yes, it's come to that, hasn't it?'

His heart skipped a beat. For every time she insisted that she was happy in her role as a vicar's wife, there were these alarming moments. Her life before meeting him had been so full, even dangerous at times. Always an open book, that's what he'd been told about himself, and apparently his face betrayed him now.

'Stop worrying, Stephen. I was just making an observation, no need to imagine that I'll pack a case and slip away when you're at the council meeting tomorrow morning.'

'That's quite a vision. That was meant to put me at ease, was it?'

'My apologies. I love you and, whilst this village is a tad boring, I love our life here too.'

'And I love you. I'd be at sea without you.'

'I was telling you about Lady Ranson. Apparently, she's getting over the fact that her precious boy is marrying a local girl.'

He knew that her intuition never erred. 'Oh? Well, that's right and good. Oliver snagged a good girl, there. Nice looking and hard working. I can't think why any family wouldn't want her.' Then he supposed maybe he was missing something. He often did. 'You do agree, don't you?'

His gorgeous wife laughed and ran a hand through her long dark hair. 'Why, yes. I adore Willa.'

She picked up her book. The title was obviously less than enriching. He knew that she always read her morning devotional, but her guilty pleasure was found in consuming stacks of paperback thrillers. Since the village library had closed, the books began arriving at an astounding rate in the post. And he would never ask her to put them aside if there was a chance that they subdued an itch for the more stimulating days of her past. But he wasn't above interrupting her reading.

'Veronica?'

Her eyes meet his.

'Let's slip upstairs now, and I'll make us that coffee afterwards.'

The cat meowed her displeasure at being unceremoniously dumped from Veronica's lap onto the floor.

CHAPTER 9

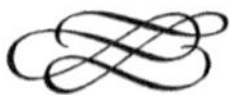

The following morning, her nerve hadn't held, so she stayed sequestered in her room at the B&B. Even though it meant giving up painting in her studio, she was too frightened that Roman may return to risk visiting the property. She thought of getting up to dress. Instead, she hid beneath the covers of the big downy bed and cried. She couldn't have said exactly why. Certainly, she'd felt threatened by Roman's behaviour and the several purple bruises on her neck; yet her tears felt like grieving.

Her eyes swollen from weeping, Elena tried to figure out the next step. She hadn't been very good at making lists, so she reviewed her situation mentally.

What can Roman and Nichola actually do? Kidnap me? Lock me away and force me to make more art for them to sell? Blackmail me?

All of these were possible, but most were unlikely.

And if most of these scenarios were unlikely, then why was she so upset?

She picked up the remote and turned on the television, hoping things would look better the following day.

. . .

MERCIFULLY, the next day brought a surge of hope—and another headache, but this time she knew it was from a lack of food and insufficient sleep. She rang downstairs and asked for her breakfast on a tray. Undoubtedly, her hostess was none too pleased, but she couldn't face making conversation with other guests. And, truly, she felt poorly.

She'd managed to get her teeth cleaned when a quiet knock came at the door. Opening the door, she recognised the proprietor's daughter and took the tray from her. Elena brought the tray to the bed and had a moment of guilt when she saw the evidence of her last food in bed. She wondered how to remove the chocolate stain on the duvet before checking out.

And when would that be?

Logically, she ought to move into her new cottage as soon as the essential deliveries arrived. They were scheduled to arrive today. She tucked into the breakfast. Draining the last of her tea, the headache began to subside. After moving the tray to the desk in the corner, she picked up the thread of her previous thoughts.

Subjecting her fears to common sense, she realised should Roman be planning a kidnapping or other violence against her, he'd have to consider Bryan Barker too. The fact that she wasn't completely unknown in this part of the world gave her some feeling of security.

She hummed old songs as she got dressed. Music had long been her friend during countless hours in the studio. Elena took her breakfast tray downstairs, stood it on the dining table, and made her way outside to her car. The skies were cloudy, but it wasn't raining. A lovely feeling of excitement came over her as her tyres rolled up the drive. She ignored the house, its tall presence still intimidating, and parked close to the cottages. Like a child, she skipped down the path between the cherry trees to her studio. There, she gave herself over to her painting for several hours. She had just stopped for a break when she saw the delivery van arrive. Walking quickly to meet him, she wondered why she had wasted so much time yesterday wallowing in the dark and hiding under the bedclothes.

'Elena Dalca?' The delivery man looked up from a handheld device. She nodded and signed for the half-dozen boxes that he moved off his van. She stowed them in her cottage and anticipated opening them later. This afternoon she wanted to continue work on her latest painting.

HUMMING AGAIN and ready for a late afternoon break, she pulled on her jumper, left the studio, and walked towards the house. The memory of Roman standing next to her in the drive gave her a moment of anxiety, but she brushed it away. She sat in the empty kitchen on the floor, enjoying the warmth of the range, with a small pot of tea and marmite on toast.

She finished the last of the tea. It had been a shock to learn Roman had been following her every move through receipts sent to her email account. On the other hand, seeing him had clarified things. She now had a new email account and had changed all of her passwords. Even though he knew where she was, it was gratifying to realise he'd made a mistake in revealing how he'd been keeping track of her.

However, it dawned on her that she would have to take serious steps to be free. Réka Lupei had somehow gained permission to bring her to England. No doubt handsome sums had changed hands, but with whom? Someone in the government? Elena had been in the "temporary" custody of Roman and Nichola for over a decade. That meant all three --Roman, Nichola, and the Wolf-- had always had access to her personal information even though she wasn't related to any of them. They had held her birth certificate, passport, personal tax accounts, and National Insurance number. These people could attempt to go on controlling her.

There seemed no way to begin again short of completely changing her identity.

There was nowhere to hide.

She simply must live her life and deal with whatever came.

As she stood up to rinse the tea things in the sink, she heard a knock on the front door. She wasn't expecting any further deliveries today.

Panic seized her.

Elena darted into the darkness of the pantry. A moment later, she heard another muffled knock.

She had left her mobile in the studio. What to do? Then it came to her: if Roman were at the front door, he'd hardly knock and patiently wait. He'd have already found the door unlocked and come through.

Elena tiptoed to the hall.

She opened the front door to a very beautiful woman, maybe in her late thirties or early forties. The lady wore a dress knitted from a silky bronze yarn, a long cream-coloured coat, and a dazzling smile.

'Hullo,' she sang. 'I hope I haven't come at a bad time?'

'Uh, no, not at all.'

'I'm Mrs Hayward, the vicar's wife from Marris Mynd. But please,' she said, holding out her leather-gloved hand, 'call me Veronica.'

'How do you do? Please'—she gestured—'come in. I'm... Elena Dalca.' Giving her real name felt liberating, like a good omen. Too bad Bryan Barker wasn't here to witness the declaration.

'Miss Dalca, what a pleasure. Oh, I see the place is still quite empty. The Smiths didn't leave a stick, did they?'

'I'm sorry there's no place to sit. They did, actually. I mean, they left iron bed frames in the cottages. In fact, I'm doing one up.'

'Are you? What a marvellous idea. Cosy, yes? I haven't been in either of the cottages before.'

Elena decided that she very much liked Veronica, the vicar's wife. Since they were standing in an empty house, she said, 'Would you like to see?'

'I would!' They laughed together and Elena retrieved the heavy iron key to the cottages. As they stepped off the gravel drive, Veronica's high-heeled shoes sunk into the soft grass and she instinctively took Elena's arm to keep herself from toddling off balance. Elena didn't mind. It was rather extraordinary how agreeable and fun it was to have Veronica here, in contrast to the sheer horror she'd felt walking leisurely over the same spot where Roman had frightened her.

Elena opened the cottage door and felt a tinge of regret. The deliveries had been hastily pushed in earlier.

'These are the things I've ordered, but I haven't had time to sort them out,' she said.

Veronica wanted to see them. 'Oh, isn't this sweet?' she said, picking up Elena's earthenware lamp by the neck.

'I hoped to get another of those, but they'd sold out of them.'

'I can see why; it's darling.'

They rummaged through the deliveries. Elena described her plans for how she would live in the cottage and where she planned to put the various items that currently made a heap in front of the fireplace.

'It'll be lovely, Elena.'

Elena grinned sheepishly. She'd been talking non-stop.

'What is it?' Veronica tilted her head. 'You seem…surprised.'

'I suppose I am. I've never done anything like this. I've never really had my own space before, beyond a studio.'

'And here was me, thinking you'd sublimely decorated all sorts of little pied-à-terre all over France, where you lived a bohemian existence, painting the local children!'

They laughed together again.

Ten minutes later, Veronica said that she'd best be on her way. They walked back towards the empty house.

'It was fabulous meeting you, Elena. And if you'd like, do drop by for our ten-thirty service. You've seen the church in Marris Mynd? We live at the vicarage in the high street. Ring me if you need anything, won't you?' Veronica handed a card to Elena that listed mobile numbers for both she and the vicar, a Stephen Hayward, alongside the church's address and service information.

'Thank you for coming,' Elena said. 'I didn't really know anyone except my estate agent.'

'Well, now you know me, and I know nearly everyone else. Do look me up when you come to the village, all right?'

Veronica turned and gave Elena a glamorous little wave as she got into her vehicle.

STEPHEN HAYWARD HAD JUST FINISHED SPREADING fresh mulch around his roses. He doted on them like children, fussing over their feeding and coddling them against the weather. He felt out of sorts when it was time to prune them, telling his wife that he despised savagely snipping their stems, but, for the good of the roses, it must be done. Because of Stephen's love of being outdoors in his garden, Veronica rarely cut roses for the house. Floral arrangements simply antagonised him.

He followed his wife into the house for a cup of tea. The house was very old, like the church itself, and very stylish, like its mistress. Veronica hung up her cream-coloured coat and he followed her down the ancient corridor into their sunny kitchen. She put the kettle on the hob.

Stephen knew about her errand and was interested to hear what had happened. Yesterday, she'd told him all about her first encounter with Elena Dalca's work.

'Do you remember when I last went to stay with Diana? That

first long break when Katie was home from university, the summer before last?'

Stephen did remember. He didn't like being on his own, but he knew how much Veronica looked forward to spending time with her only sister and niece.

'Well, we'd gone to a special exhibit at the art museum, and Elena Dalca's paintings were part of it. Oh, Stephen, her work is just gorgeous. I was so in awe of her painting, "Madonna's Tears." But that wasn't even the most beautiful. I remember coming face to face with her famous landscape, "Provencal Play." The one with the lovely French children in the fields that she'd painted when she was only nine. It was breathtaking.'

It was then that Veronica remembered a book she'd purchased at the museum shop. She located it on the shelf and showed it to him. 'Here she is, darling. Our new neighbour.' She tapped a photograph while he adjusted his reading glasses.

She was a pretty girl with expressive dark eyes and long dark hair, quite like his wife's; slight in build and quite fragile-looking. 'She isn't very sturdy to be painting such monstrous canvases.'

Veronica smiled. 'Yes, I thought the same. Such depth of feeling and such mastery for a person so young.'

The kettle whistled just as Veronica stood a pair of mugs, white with red poppies up the sides on the table. She didn't eat sweets, but she pulled a piece of shortbread from the packet for Stephen.

Stephen had been in favour of reaching out to the girl, in case she found herself in need of assistance. He asked, 'Do you suppose she was suspicious of you?'

'No,' Veronica answered. 'I startled her, of course. She probably thought I was acting like a nosy vicar's wife, charging onto her property and being overtly friendly. But I felt we connected rather well. If she suspected--or knew--that Roman Giblin was asking after her, then I think she would've felt comfortable mentioning it. Somehow, I think she's like us; wondering what he's up to and what he's going to do next. At any rate, she didn't voice any concerns, short of questioning her naive judgement in acquiring such a massive house alongside the cottages and studio, the latter of which are perfect for her.'

Stephen bit into his biscuit. He chewed thoughtfully. 'Well, at least she knows we're here for her should he come back.' What he really meant was that Veronica was there for her. Because of her past, Veronica was a formidable opponent.

'Yes, that's something, I suppose. And I've already come up with a brilliant idea for that property of hers.'

Stephen grinned, duly proud of his wife and her sensible schemes. 'The poor child. Do let her get settled first, Veronica.'

CHAPTER 10

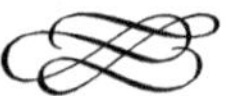

Willa Purslow had a busy day ahead. Since leaving cookery school, she worked four long days each week at the tea room in Church Stretton. Her brother-in-law, Rhys, had made it all possible by lending her his pickup truck to drive to and from work. He insisted he didn't miss having access to his own truck, but once she'd overheard him and Mollie sorting out their schedule. They obviously would have an easier time if they didn't have to share the farm's old Land Rover. But when Willa had tried to make other arrangements, they wouldn't hear of it.

'It takes a little coordinating on our part, but it's quite manageable to have you driving the truck,' Mollie had said. 'Honestly, Willa.'

Rhys had agreed. Willa had hugged them both and thanked them, again. It was, for now, the most practical solution for her meagre salary.

She and Oliver were planning a simple wedding. But getting married from his family's formidable country house saw her considering more expensive catering than she would've chosen for a modest reception in the village hall.

In the cramped tea room kitchen, Willa waited for her timer to ring, twirling her long blonde ponytail around her finger. It was fortunate that she could virtually bake in her sleep, because wedding details slipped into her thoughts morning, noon, and night. She went to the ovens to retrieve the coconut cakes, then set aside the ingredients for the scones.

The owner of the tea room, Roni, had allowed Willa to design seasonal menus. A changing menu had been something that the cafe hadn't offered before Willa joined the staff. Her current menu for March offered some hearty favourites, including buttery shortbread, sweet and spicy ginger cake, and zesty lemon scones. She'd also encouraged Roni to serve more local produce, including some of Rhys' vegetables, fresh Shropshire-made butter, and honey from a beekeeper in nearby Chelmick. Customers loved the variety, and the tea room's figures showed a substantial increase.

Willa had just finished placing the scones on the baking sheet when one of the waiting staff, Nancy, came in for her apron.

'I think I could gain a stone from merely smelling your baking, Willa.'

'Go on, then.'

'Really?' Nancy exclaimed, excited as a child. A too-small piece of shortbread was loosely wrapped in kitchen paper and Willa nodded towards it.

'Ooo, no, wait. I'm going to make a cuppa and sit down and enjoy it. I've got ten minutes before my shift begins.' Nancy put a small amount of water in a kettle and dropped it on the hob. The staff kept personal mugs on a small shelf, and she took hers down. It was ocean blue and was labelled "I (heart) Pen-y-Dyffryn Hotel" on the side. Everyone knew that was where she and Gary had spent their honeymoon in Oswestry three years ago.

Willa smiled at her and gently pushed the baking sheets into the oven. She would do a bit of washing up to give the coconut cake more time to cool before she frosted it.

'How's Charley?'

'Oh, Willa, he's such a love. His colic is finally gone and we all of us got some sleep last night. You'll see when you have your own wee ones how much you value basic bodily functions. I didn't get a bath on my day off; he was that fussy.'

'I'm so glad he's better. See, you deserve that shortbread, don't you?'

'You know, I really do!' Nancy said, sitting down with her cup of tea. She put her toes up on the edge of a stainless steel rack that stood against the wall.

'And you, Willa. We haven't had a chance to chat. How're your wedding plans coming on?'

'It's difficult to say. Just when I think I've considered everything, I see something on the checklist I've forgotten about. Or someone asks me about something and I realise I've been completely scatty. And then when I go to make a decision, I'm completely overcome by choice. I never knew there were so many fonts to choose from for the invites!'

Nancy laughed and nodded her head in agreement.

Willa continued, 'The other day, Roni asked me whether I was borrowing my mum's cake topper or did I buy new? And I said, "What?" I'd totally forgotten. And I'm a *baker!*'

They laughed again, and Nancy took the last bite of shortbread. Willa gathered the three ingredients for making the icing. Her fluffy, white seven-minute frosting, garnished with pieces of grated coconut over the top, had been the first cake in the fifteen-year history of the tea room to sell out during the lunch service. Needless to say, Willa had made dozens of them in the last two-and-a-half years.

'So, have you decided where you're going to live yet? I guess I've forgotten if you said whether you're staying here or if Oliver has a job elsewhere.'

'That's all up in the air at the moment,' Willa said cheerfully. She iced the cake even faster than usual, as though illustrating how little time there was to consider such things. 'Oliver has so much on his mind…'

'Oh, well…' Nancy looked away, as though she felt uncomfortable with the situation Willa found herself in.

'And of course, I haven't decided what I would like to do, either, which isn't helping. You know, it's only been a few weeks since I got my cookery certificate.'

'At least you have a good place here, even if he hasn't figured out what he'd like to do. Well, I suppose I'd best get to it.' Nancy quickly rinsed her mug and slipped away.

Willa stood back from her iced cake and wondered what Nancy had thought. Clearly, people were as confused as she was by Oliver's lack of plans. Perhaps they thought something even worse, that Oliver didn't really intend to marry her. She never wore her diamond engagement ring when working in the kitchen. Willa grunted aloud. Well, it shouldn't matter what other people think.

Even if he hadn't given much thought to what they were going to do after they married in June. Or where they were going to live. *How* they were going to live.

Or, seemingly, anything else at all.

She threw her spatula in the sink and sighed.

Elena was disappointed to find that the library in Marris Mynd had closed. She looked through the window with cupped hands around her eyes. She had expected to be cutting it fine since the evening was creeping in, but it wasn't the hour.

The library was completely empty. Permanently shut.

She felt a surprising level of disappointment. She was lonely today, and the vacant building echoed the emptiness inside. It must've been a beautiful library. And in such a stately, very old building as well.

'I agree. It was gorgeous.'

Elena jumped. She turned to find a young girl, possibly in her early teens. The girl would be best described as ordinary, with a thick body, short legs, and mousy-coloured hair. There was a sweet openness to her expression. She straddled a rusty old bicycle and waited for Elena to respond, keen to have a chat.

'Yes, I imagine that it was lovely. How long ago did it close?'

'About two-and-a-half years ago. It took my very best friend with it.'

Elena was drawn in by the girl's factual attitude and curious statement.

'What'd you mean, exactly?' Elena asked, envisioning some horrible accident inside the ancient building involving collapsing ceilings.

The plain girl sighed and stepped her leg over the bike and leaned it against her hip. 'My best friend forever, Phoebe. Her mum was the librarian here my whole life. Then they closed the library. Next thing I knew, Phoebe's mum had a new job and then married him—married her boss, you see. And now they live at his house in Ludlow, which might as well be the Hebrides if you can't drive a car and have no money for the bus.'

'I'm sorry to hear that. So Phoebe never returns to Marris Mynd?'

'She does actually, sometimes. She has two sisters here. One is called Willa and she's very nice. And the other one, Mollie, is married, so there's Phoebe's brother-in-law, too. He's Welsh. The three of them live in the big farmhouse at the top of our hill. But Phoebe has...moved on.'

'I'm Elena.'

'I know.'

'You do?'

'Yes, miss. Everyone knows who you are.'

The girl smiled, and Elena realised she was probably a girl with keen intelligence, despite the way she constantly pushed her glasses back up to the bridge of her pugged nose. She lumbered forward, one hand left behind on the bicycle, the other extended in greeting. 'I'm Charlotte Seabury. I'm your neighbour. We're the house that sits just below yours, with the white gate by the drive.'

It felt odd to meet someone who had been aware of her all of the time, practically living on her doorstep. Elena said, 'I know exactly the gate you mean.'

'My friend, Phoebe? Her family--the sisters and Rhys--are at Hilltop Farm. Opposite the road from us, upon the crest of the hill. Perhaps since it's past your place, you haven't been up there?'

'No, I haven't. I've only come down, past your gate, to Marris Mynd. Then on to Church Stretton and all around, you know.'

'Not to Ludlow, though, where Phoebe lives?'

'No. I'm sure it's very nice.'

'I've visited a few times. But even if I could get to Ludlow, Phoebe doesn't want me 'round anymore. She's very popular at her school.'

'Oh.' Elena could think of nothing to say. She'd never really had a best friend at Charlotte and Phoebe's age. By then, she'd worked a lot, sometimes to the point where her tutor became frustrated with her lack of focus on schoolwork. Several tutors had quit, and she hadn't finished secondary school. Taking her GCSEs hadn't even been a thought, with her travelling all over the world for exhibitions.

'My apologies for moaning. I'm not bitter or anything, it's just the way Phoebe is.' Charlotte thumbed her glasses higher on her nose. 'And I happened to be thinking about her, and her family, and how the library used to be here. And how things change, and people move out of your life. I suppose I got a bit melancholic.'

Elena smiled. 'I've felt that emotion a lot lately. In fact, I came to the village just to cheer myself up.'

'Really?' This amazed the girl. 'And do you feel better, even though you found the library closed forever?'

'I do. Because I met you, Charlotte.'

They shared another smile. Elena thought the girl was lovely. An unlikely friend, but a welcome one. So she said, 'How about you show me the high street? Then we'll put your bicycle in the back, and I'll drop you home?'

Charlotte was beaming. 'Brill!'

SINCE HER CONVERSATION at the tea room kitchen with Nancy, Willa had stressed about all sorts of horrors that were no doubt bubbling beneath the surface of her relationship with Oliver. She didn't want to discuss it over the phone. She needed to look into his eyes.

She'd told her sister, Mollie, who'd been good mates with Oliver.

'You're being so grim, Willa,' Mollie declared. 'If Oliver wanted to, he'd just break things off. But he keeps ringing from university and telling you he loves you. You're getting married. Why are you so upset?'

Willa hadn't answered. The truth was, she and Oliver had had a terrific row during their last phone conversation.

'I need to know, Oliver, what our plans are,' she'd told him.

'Not today. You know how hard I'm working on preparing for my oral examination.'

Ordinarily, Willa wasn't one to sulk. But she couldn't seem to stop pressing him. She felt possessed. Sometimes, she hardly recognised herself since she'd begun wedding planning. 'I'm simply asking you, Oliver, what will become of my life in three months' time, and you can't be bothered to answer me.'

Oliver had grown quiet. She knew he was trying to control his temper as she heard him release a sigh into the phone. She loathed herself, but felt driven to prise answers from him. *Now.*

He'd been so concerned about his mother being a prude toward her, but it was Oliver that Willa was angry with.

His voice was tight. 'Because I don't know, sweetie. All right?'

'It isn't all right, actually. You've had over two years to think about our future, and you never want to make plans. I am *still* part of your plans, right?'

'Willa, why are you behaving this way? We're going to marry in June, and we can have long talks about all of this as soon as I finish here. For the moment, those plans should suffice.'

Her anger became fear. She hadn't intended to make him so cross.

'I love you, Oliver. I'm sorry.' She'd started tearing up, which somehow made her compulsive again. 'But people are asking me if I'll be continuing on at the tea room and I don't even have a clue.' Her whining gave way to sobs. 'I mean...at this point, I'm imagining myself being married to you but living on my own here at the farm. You haven't given me any other scenario to hope for! I've no idea where we're even meant to live!'

Oh, God, why am I unable to stop? She knew being half-hysterical would solve nothing. She'd literally clamped her teeth down on her lip.

There was silence for a moment at the other end of the phone. Then he'd said, 'I've told you before, whether or not you want to work and where you want to work is completely your decision.'

She realised he had, in fact, said that last bit before. But she needed *something*. 'But you don't have any opinion at all?' She heard herself shouting, 'In my mind, Oliver, that translates to one thing. You don't care. You're not interested in what I do, or how I spend my time. How can I believe that you care about me when you won't take an interest in my work? I'm interested in your education. In fact, I'm bloody curious to the point of madness to know what you intend doing with your life.' More tears. She didn't know whether to hate herself or Oliver more.

'Willa?'

'Yes,' she'd mumbled, tears still tracking down her face.

'I'm sorry, baby, but I must get on. I'll ring you in a couple of days.'

'All right.'

And then he was gone. Without saying he loved her, like he always had done before they rang off.

Was this somehow a warning? Would marrying Oliver be the biggest mistake of her life? She wasn't sure that the differences in their families, and—dare she say it,their difference in class—could be overcome. It was one of those rare moments where she wondered if her thoughts would be different, somehow, had she known her own father. What would he say about Oliver's indifference? Willa dropped across her bed and lay there for hours, lost in thought.

CHAPTER 11

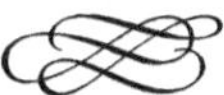

The following morning, Willa awoke regretful that she'd behaved so childishly over the phone. Oliver had a massive job of work to do, and she ought to be supportive until he finished. But, still, she felt that her questions were reasonable ones that any bride would want answers to.

From bed, she reached out to her small table for one of her books to hold for comfort.

She wasn't scheduled to work at the bakery for the next several days. Oliver hadn't offered any suggestions regarding her job. Perhaps that was a good place to start; she should think about work. But a few minutes later, she'd come back around to the same point: how could she make a decision about her job if she didn't even know if they'd stay in the area? Some of Oliver's practical experience courses had been spent in London, some in Scotland. Would he want to return to either of those? For all she knew, he was thinking about moving to another country.

Willa turned onto her side in her warm little bed.

Her thoughts strayed back to several years ago. Mollie had been very upset. She had broken up with Rhys, and, at the time, it had seemed permanent. Ironically, Mollie had talked to Oliver about it and felt a lot better.

But who could *she* turn to? Mollie knew Oliver, but Mollie was so different in her thinking. Her sister wouldn't understand. Mollie was one of the fortunate ones. She'd always known what she wanted to do. In fact, she'd inherited her dream. She carried on doing what their dad had taught her, keeping goats and being a farmer. Mollie had achieved his dream of making artisan cheeses. Willa wished she was like her sister; Mollie seemed to possess an inner homing device; she lived from her heart and always knew what to do.

At school, Willa had been told that she was very bright, but she found intelligence didn't always point towards what a person actually ought to *do*. She certainly didn't feel clever when it came to making plans. It was only because of an insightful remark from the vicar's wife, Veronica Hayward, that Willa had taken up cookery courses. Without Veronica's guidance, Willa would still be milking goats every morning with Mollie.

Willa sat up and found that she had a massive headache. She walked gingerly to the loo, and then downstairs.

As she filled the kettle from the tap, the door to the boot room opened. She heard her sister come through and stop to kick off her gum boots.

Mollie called, 'Add some water for mine, would you?'

'Like I wouldn't already know.'

'What's wrong with you?' Mollie said, coming into the kitchen with straw clinging to her jeans. It scattered onto the floor—the floor Willa had cleaned last night.

Willa put the kettle on the hob and leaned against it. She crossed her arms and slowly dropped her head back, gazing at the ceiling. Her head pounded slightly less violently in this position. 'I had an awful row with Oliver.'

'Trouble in paradise, huh? What happened, did one of you forget to say please or thank you?'

Willa levelled her chin and looked at her older sister. 'Very amusing. I didn't have a go at you when you and Rhys had issues.'

'That's true. Sorry, Willis.'

'Don't call me that. I've never said, but I don't like it when you call me that.'

'Okaaayyy,' Mollie said, raising her hands defensively. 'You know what you need?'

Willa gave her a look, warning her. *'What?'*

'A visit to Granny.'

Granny. How had she not thought of Granny? 'That, Mollie, is an absolute corker.'

'Why not take your tea upstairs and get something for your head? Yes, it's that obvious.' Mollie pulled her mobile from the pocket of her jeans. 'I'll ring Granny and set up a visit, all right?'

'You're a star.'

'I know.'

WILLA SAT in her grandmother's elegant drawing room in the smart environs of Sutton Coldfield, Birmingham. The large house inhabited over an acre of lawn and gardens, edged by a tree-lined, quiet street. Except for the ticking of the great clock in the hall, the heavy plush carpeting and double-glazing coddled Granny's house in tranquillity.

The lack of ambient noise was a stark contrast to Willa's blubbering.

'I am so sorry, Granny.' She snuffled. Willa was the most reserved of her family, which made her recent outbursts all the more humiliating. 'I don't imagine for a moment that Oliver doesn't love me. I shall marry him. But I'm at a total loss. He simply seems incapable of *caring.*'

Granny Phoebe, after whom Willa's younger sister was called, reached across the settee and patted Willa's knee. 'Darling, I must say, I think you're overreacting a bit.'

Willa was shocked. Surely Granny wasn't taking Oliver's side?

'But I'm not, Granny. I mean, I've been patient for over *two years,* never pressing Oliver about our plans. During holidays, I knew he ought to relax. I've not even pestered him about wedding decisions because he's needed to concentrate on finishing his doctorate.'

Granny's face was immovable.

Maybe she ought to have gone to her mum's house instead? Her mum didn't usually have the best advice, she was more of the *c'est la vie* type of person. But at least she'd be...compassionate.

'Your words, lamb, not mine.' Granny smoothed a strand of her gloriously white bobbed hair behind her ear and looked pointedly at Willa.

'Sorry?' Willa said, dabbing her nose with a tissue.

'You said you hadn't been pressing him. Clearly, you are. Perhaps at the most inopportune time.'

Willa's hands trembled slightly and she felt a deep blush warm her cheeks. Willa wasn't sure she could cope simultaneously with Oliver's indifference and Granny's cruelty. Still, Granny Phoebe's good advice was legendary, and Willa longed to make changes. Whatever it took to stop her feeling so wretched.

'All right, Granny. Obviously, you think I've got it all wrong. But that's why I'm here, isn't it? To figure out what I ought to do.'

Granny smiled. Willa smiled in return, inwardly repenting for thinking her grandmother cruel.

'Willa, it's quite simple, really. In Britain, we deny the issue of class and we claim it doesn't matter. And much of the time, it doesn't. It's largely an outmoded concept and we strive to prove social stratum is irrelevant by treating everyone as well as we can. I'm very happy to deal with people of any background who are well-intentioned, courteous, and generous of spirit.'

Willa felt pride in her grandmother. Although Granny was not a person to be trifled with, she wasn't a snob. In all her life, she'd never heard Granny abuse one of her employees--correct them, yes, as any employer might; a bit sharply sometimes, but that was according to Granny's temperament, not her bank account--and she certainly didn't play the Lady of the Manor.

Willa's thoughts flew to Oliver's mother. Perhaps Colleen really hadn't been guilty of being condescending towards Willa? Perhaps when she snapped at Willa, it was because she was worried about her husband and couldn't, at the moment, truly remember what it was that Willa did. It wasn't as though Willa had ever invited Colleen to the tea room where she worked, or even spoke about her job.

'I agree, Granny. Most people—the ones you care to know, anyway—seek to minimise the differences with other people. Wherever they find themselves in the social order of things.'

But what had any of this to do with she and Oliver?, a fiancé who wouldn't communicate? She figured it was definitely a women-and-men thing.

'Yet, you'll have to accept, my dear, that you're marrying a young man of great fortune,' Granny continued. 'As such, he's been raised with a different mindset. You're a bright girl, Willa; you must see differences between, say, Rhys and Oliver?'

'Of course, Granny. But, class aside, they're completely different people. Oliver doesn't take an interest in me. He's been saying things like he doesn't mind if I work or not. What does he expect me to do if I don't work? To just be a...nothing?'

Granny arched an eyebrow. 'Like his mother?'

Willa was struck silent. It wasn't quite fair.

Willa thought of Colleen as busy and industrious. She always had important projects demanding her time. Yet, she was Lady Ranson, mostly. She didn't have a career, so to speak, outside her home. But Colleen was a really great mother and a vital volunteer. Her life was hardly nothing. Willa thoughtfully pulled the tassel of the cushion that lay beside her on the sofa.

'Remember this, Willa. It's only the really grand who never seriously contemplate these things, they simply work hard to contribute their ability in the roles they're given. And the way they advance through life is a bit different. Oliver was born the first and only son, the heir of Myndcroft Hall. His responsibilities are clear from the beginning. Because he already has a *purpose.* From birth. He's to always keep in mind the stewardship of his home, to consider those who depend on him for a living, and to benefit his community. He must go to a proper school and get an education to inform his decisions. And if he's wonderfully lucky, he finds not only a girl who is suitable--meaning, mature--but that he loves and genuinely enjoys spending his time with. He's about to accomplish one of the biggest goals of his life, and surely he's delighted to have his relationship with you. He must be thinking what a stroke of luck.'

Willa giggled. 'He actually said that once. "I'm the luckiest man in the world to have discovered the girl next door." Isn't that charming?'

Granny smiled and gave her a pat. 'It shows his good sense.'

'Everything you've said is right, Granny. And I agree about Oliver's life being clear cut. Like Mollie's. But I'm asking about me. How do I fit in, and why doesn't he care?'

'His role, his mindset, is how he looks at your life, Willa. We're all from our own little planet, and we see others from that point of view. Decisions like where you choose to live may seem like small details when you hold vast property, Willa. And your career is peripheral at the moment. This is something for you to consider, as Oliver's mother has typically made her own decisions--can you imagine her husband having the time to decide for her what ought to be done at the Shropshire Women's Aid committee meetings?'

Willa shook her head. It was beginning to make sense, but it hadn't quite come together for her.

Granny continued, 'What matters to Oliver is *family.* And with the confidence he's had in himself, in his circumstances, he allows himself to do one thing at a time. You'll find, darling, that most men don't multitask. Undoubtedly, Oliver is comfortable believing that you'll talk together and sort out what you'd like to do *later.* After he accomplishes this great scholarly goal that he's given himself, and after you're married. As Churchill said, my dear, "It is a mistake to try to look too far ahead. The chain of destiny can only be grasped one link at a time."'

Willa scooted over closer to her grandmother and leaned her head upon Phoebe's shoulder. 'Why have I been so horrible to him, Granny? Because I actually agree with all of that. I think family, and looking after all of those things that his family is blessed to have, is important. I don't have any problems with those priorities, and I've been simply awful towards him.'

'Darling, there's always a learning curve.'

'It's not that he doesn't care, then, Granny? It isn't that he doesn't value my job, but it's that Oliver's perspective is different, and he's been working towards his doctorate for...*years.* He just wants to finish. And he just wants me to find my own place, because only I know my own mind, right? So, I'm to work where I choose and let the future stay in the future, at least for the moment.'

'I did say you were an intelligent girl.'

Willa leaned in to meet her wise grandmother in an embrace. Granny kissed the top of Willa's head and then suggested they go out for supper at Ristorante Da Gino.

CHAPTER 12

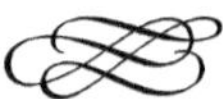

New ideas of how to take control of her career came to her in the shower. Excited, Elena postponed shampooing her hair in order to get dried off and pick up her mobile. She rang her estate agent--or rather, his son--hoping to get a referral.

'Bryan? Hello, it's Elena Dalca.'

'Miss Tansy Button, how are things at the big house?'

They laughed.

'I'm settling in the loft cottage.'

'Finding your inner nester, are you?'

'Yes. And I've made a new acquaintance, the vicar's wife.'

'Ah, the lady that looks more like Catherine Zeta-Jones?'

Elena giggled. 'She does! She's very easy to talk to, so I told her my ideas for the cottage. Before she left, she told me the best place to buy curtains.'

'Before I even got the chance.'

'But I do need a referral, actually. Would you happen to know anyone who designs logos and websites?'

Bryan said, 'Well, not nearly as thrilling as curtains, but you're in luck. My mate will do a top-notch job for you. If you look over his website, you'll see he's done a number of other websites. You'll probably agree that they look really great.'

'I suppose it wouldn't matter to your friend if I don't have a clue what I want?'

'No, it wouldn't matter. He'll be able to work up something for you to look at.'

'I don't mean to be mysterious, Bryan, so I'll just explain, shall I?'

'You know that isn't necessary--'

'I know, but you've been so kind to me. You're already well aware, of course, of my problems with my former guardian, Roman Giblin and his wife, Nichola. I've been thinking that if I'm to manage my own career as an artist, then I ought to have my own website. This way, people could contact me directly, perhaps even shop online. What do you reckon?'

'Of course, that makes perfect sense. Congratulations to you, coming along on your own. I'm sending on my mate's contact information. Take a look at his website; he has lots of samples of his work, and that may give you ideas about how you'll want your work to feature too. All right, love?'

'Perfect.'

They rang off. Elena hastily followed the link. Bryan's mate was called Dashiell Minton. Elena scanned some of the website pages and was impressed with his work. The pages had a clean, modern style, but also managed to convey a sense of the person or business. She clicked the "About" page and found that Dashiell Minton had studied art at a prestigious school. There was a small black and white photo of him. Dark, wavy hair and a strong, masculine jaw. He was wearing a leather jacket and was rather slim but broad-shouldered. His eyes appeared light; perhaps blue, green, or grey? She lingered on the photo of him for longer than she'd care to admit and was about to hit the "Contact" page and send Dashiell Minton a message when she noticed a connected page she'd not yet visited. It was titled

"Organic Expressions." She clicked the tab and was shifted onto another site.

Dashiell Minton's second website, showcasing his career as a fine artist.

She studied the collage of sculptures he'd made of metal and the sepia-toned photos of the young man welding iron. There was an old-fashioned "letter" in a font that appeared hand-written. She glanced at the bottom where the digital letter was signed by the artist.

It read:

My day job is to create homes on the internet for my clients. It's enjoyable to collaborate with people and to help them present and package their thoughts, goods, and services. If I can serve you in that way, please reach out.

But aside from my day job, my passion is to work with raw materials as a mixed media artist. I find myself drawn to rendering organic shapes and discovering fresh narratives from metal, wood, and clay. This is my true vocation, my deepest soul expression as an artist. Whilst I create for myself initially, it's enormously satisfying when others find joy in the finished creation. If you've kindly taken the time to view my online gallery, I'd love to have a comment from you. If you find a piece in the gallery that particularly speaks to you, please reach out through the contact page for availability and pricing.

~Dashiell Minton

ELENA FELT a kinship with this artist and his love for his work. Aside from the fact that he was gorgeous and she hoped to learn he was single, there certainly couldn't be a better choice of person for doing her website. He would understand what was needed and be able to digitally interpret her personality in a tasteful way.

She sent a message to his graphic design website and looked forward to his response.

Elena put her paintbrush down and stepped back to survey her painting. A peaceful feeling settled over her when a work was finished; trying to bring it along further would cause the composition to fail. She had learnt the boundaries of completion by ruining a number of paintings.

She shrugged out of her large denim work shirt and left the studio, walking the path between the cherry trees, crossing the drive, and then the lawn to arrive at her cottage. The painting had been a wonderful journey. It had commanded her attention until after midnight several nights in a row and then called to her before dawn. In the coming week, she knew an empty feeling would come, pushing her to begin the next work.

But for the moment, Elena was done in.

She dropped a teabag into her mug and poured freshly boiled water over it. The scented steam caressed her face. Everything seemed beautiful today. Magical.

Meeting Charlotte in the village had been the only people-facing interaction she'd had in a week. Charlotte wanted to introduce Elena to her family, her closest neighbours. Perhaps now that she had finished the painting, it would be a good time to ring and set something up. She picked up her mobile and noticed that she had a message. It was from Dashiell Minton, regarding the website.

Miss Dalca,

Thank you for your enquiry. I'm due to finish a project this afternoon, and I shall begin designing your website tomorrow. When I last visited London, I saw several pieces of your brilliant work, both in galleries and museums. I have

an idea of how your website could look. Please send me a few files, including the bio you prefer (I can recommend a writer if you don't yet have that sorted) and images of your paintings. From those, I can create a sample website for you to look at, and we can discuss any changes or additions. If you have time, we could meet at the coffee shop at Pulverbridge. If not, we can manage via email or Skype. Let me know your preference. Thank you for your interest.

Dash Minton

HER PULSE RACED at the thought of meeting him in person. She reread. He suggested the meeting before the other options, so she would go with that, and try not to overthink it.

She typed: Dash.

She paused. She loved his full name, but was immediately struck by the shortened version. *Dash.* It was strong, unusual, and, well, dashing. She felt Charlotte's age, remembering what it was like to write a boy's name over and over again in an exercise book. Chiding herself to stop being silly, especially since he was most likely married with baby number three on the way, she thought of what she ought to write.

Best to be brief. Professional, but not cold. She didn't do cold.

DASH,

It's terribly embarrassing to admit this, but the only photos I have of my work are snaps that I've taken of the two paintings completed since I moved to the area. I'll send them along to serve as a "place saver" in your design. And I definitely need help with the bio; I'm pants at writing (as you can see here). Would love to meet at the coffee shop.

Thank you,

Elena

SHE SHOULD'VE WRITTEN, "Yes, I would be available to meet and discuss," or something a bit grown-up. But it was done now.

Shockingly, the mobile came to life. He'd already written back.

ELENA,

No worries, plenty of pictures of your work on the internet that I can sub in for now. Greeking (dummy text) can suffice for the bio at present. Would tomorrow at two work for you? I can have a sample to show you by then, and we'll go from there.

Best regards,

Dash

HE'D USED her first name and it thrilled her.. She really did need to get out more.

ELENA HADN'T SHOPPED for clothes in a number of years. Nichola had functioned as a sort of stylist and always had an outfit ready for her appearances at galleries, press events, or conferences. Regina, Nichola's housekeeper's daughter and her partner in crime, had donated these to the closest charity shop.

She was enjoying buying little treasures to set in the windowsills of the loft cottage, collecting new bits of pottery (she'd purchased some with Charlotte at the little gifts area of the local chemist in Marris Mynd) and choosing floor rugs weaved with exuberant colours.

But she hadn't bought any clothes. And she was meeting Dash Minton tomorrow.

Elena rummaged through her wardrobe, which was actually a collection of the rags she wore to the studio. Dash was also an artist, thus he probably had lots of working clothes. It wasn't much comfort.

It occurred to her that it had been a very long time since she'd cared what a chap would think of her appearance. This romantic concern was quite welcome.

'I THOUGHT Granny had you all sorted.' Mollie was beyond frustrated with her sister. They were having their family dinner at the table in their large kitchen at Hilltop Farm. 'I'm not sure this has anything to do with Oliver. You're acting like a proper "bridezilla."'

'Now, now. I seem to remember your getting a bit distracted,' Rhys said to his wife, with a wink at Willa. 'Am I right, sister?'

'You are,' Willa said, grateful that Rhys had brought Mollie back to smiling. He was probably the only person on the planet that could once Mollie's temper flared. Rhys, and perhaps Granny. Everything Willa said got her sister going, even if Mollie was in agreement with her.

Mollie dropped her chin and looked askance at her husband. 'You're on her side because she cooks for us.'

Rhys lifted his shoulders a bit. 'Not going to bite the hand that feeds.'

Mollie leaned over and kissed Rhys. 'Then maybe I ought to learn to cook, hmm?'

Willa interrupted. 'Hello? Can we just get through the meal first?'

'You mean, "Can we get on with talking about me and Oliver?"'

Ignoring her sister, Willa turned to Rhys. 'I know you and Oliver have different circumstances--'

'As well as different education, different socio-economic backgrounds...'

Mollie groaned. She left the table to begin the washing up.

'I'd still value your opinion, Rhys.'

'You're asking me, as a bloke, what I think.' Rhys put down his knife and fork.

Willa nodded.

'I think you're a fine cook, and I'll be sorry to lose you to Oliver.'

Willa couldn't help but smile. 'And?'

'Well, I'm thinking back to when Mollie broke up with me.'

'Excuse me?' Mollie turned around from the basin and glared at him.

'I'm thinking back to when I broke up with Mollie. My best plan at the time was to leave my dad's dairy and strike out on my own as a veggie farmer. I had a few ideas, but the *worst* thing was not being able to talk to Mollie.'

'I love you, sexy farmer man,' Mollie called out over the water splashing in the sink.

'But I'm always ready to listen to Oliver...'

'That's not what he meant,' Mollie said.

'That's not what I meant,' Rhys said. They were more than beginning to sound like one another, Willa thought. Soon, Mollie would have a Welsh accent.

'Had we not broken up and had I not had so much time on my hands, I might not've come to that idea as soon. Most blokes take things as they come, then try to sort it all out. But you're different. You're a planner, Willa.'

'I'm not, Rhys. Oliver has said it's down to me whether I should work. But I don't have a clue what's best. I haven't planned anything. That's the problem.'

'All right, love. I see. It's just that--'

The drain gurgled and Mollie walked back to the kitchen table, drying her hands on a towel. 'He means that you ought to make plans. And that if you have a good idea, pursue it. And if it includes Oliver, more's the better.'

'Precisely,' Rhys agreed.

'Granny already told you.' Mollie sat down at the table again. 'Because Ollie doesn't have a better idea at the mo anyway, and he's too busy to think about it. And, Oliver'll enjoy sharing your plans with you, Willa. When he can.'

'I started off with what I didn't want to do,' Rhys offered. 'Looking after dairy cows. Maybe if you think of what isn't working, that'll be a place to start.'

Willa took a deep breath. 'I think…well, this is embarrassing.'

'*What?*' asked her sister and brother-in-law in unison.

Talking at the same time, too, Willa thought.

'After so desperately wanting Oliver's feedback, I suddenly feel I'm past it,' Willa replied. She splayed her hands and looked at the table. 'It's only just occurred to me this very moment what *isn't* working. I've been at the tea room for a few years now. The changes I've made have been good; it's made them more money. I haven't made more money, though. And although I haven't really admitted this to myself before now, it's made me think I've outgrown them. I don't want to work at other people's businesses. I want to work on my own.'

'Wow,' Mollie said. Rhys just smiled.

Willa's eyes became the size of saucers. 'Do you think I'm being arrogant?'

'*No.*' Once again, Mr and Mrs Davies answered in chorus.

'Okay. I wasn't sure.' Willa laughed. 'I do appreciate this. It's helping.'

Rhys resumed his role of asking the questions. 'So you don't want to work at the tea room--'

'Oh, well, I'm not saying that, strictly speaking. They've been very good to me, you know. And I have wedding things to pay for.'

Mollie groaned with impatience. 'He's asking that if you've outgrown the tea room and you're going into business for yourself, then *what do you want to do?*'

Willa propped her elbows on the table and dropped her head into her hands. 'Oh, I just don't know.'

The Davies sighed in unison.

CHAPTER 13

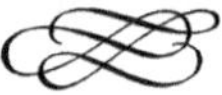

Taking control of her career proved to be rather exciting. Elena stayed in bed an extra half hour, turning over ideas in her mind, dreaming of ways to go forward with making a positive impact. Roman usually sent regrets when opportunities offered no advantage to himself. Instead, Elena considered charities that pulled at her heartstrings. In the future, she could say *yes.* It was amazing to realise she was in control. She could not only create art, but use it to help people. She was living a magical new life. It seemed as though working away in Roman's garage had happened a lifetime ago.

But for the present, her next step would be meeting with Dashiell Minton to discuss the website design. To say that she had butterflies was an understatement.

She turned her vehicle into the car park at Common Grounds, a hip coffee shop in Pulverbridge. The employees wore soft knit hats, sported tattoos, and the music exuded a cool vibe. The man she'd seen pictured online was already there, more gorgeous in person.

He stood immediately and walked towards her. 'Elena? Dash Minton. How do you do?'

He was so fit. Elena felt her cheeks flush. She hoped he wouldn't notice. As indicated from the small photo on his website, he was tall and slim, with dark hair waving deliciously in all the right directions. His eyes were sort of green, somewhat hazel. He wore a faded black shirt and dark jeans with brown leather boots.

'What will you have?'

She hadn't a clue.

'They do a good flat white; that's what I'm drinking.'

She nodded in agreement.

'Make yourself comfortable.'

You really impressed there, Elena, she thought. She sat down at the round wooden table. Its carved surface resembled a circular labyrinth. On its top was an opened laptop computer and a coffee that was already half gone. Dash's dark suede jacket was slung over the back of the chair.

Suddenly, he returned, setting down a coffee topped with a feathered design fashioned in cream. He lowered his tall body into the chair opposite to her and his spicy, woodsy cologne drifted across. Elena realised she hadn't said a word yet. She peered into her coffee, pulled a confused face, and said, 'Lovely, even though it's rendered in dairy instead of paint.'

He looked at her and then looked down.

Did he not get the joke? No, she thought, *it was just that bad.* Elena opened her mouth to apologise.

But then Dash said, 'Yes, but the *coverage* is excellent. I know because two months ago, I bashed my humongous carryall into the table and spilt coffee all over my client.'

'Oh, dear.' Elena's eyes went wide. It was so kind of him to smooth over her awkward attempt at humour.

'If only that were what the client said. I honestly thought he was burnt for a moment, but when I asked him if he needed to go to hospital, the language got very complimentary, indeed. He called me a smart arse and walked out.'

'As though he'd never made a mistake.'

'Exactly that. Later I concluded that perhaps I'd dodged a bullet in not having to work for him.'

Dash Minton took a drink of his coffee. He gave her a warm smile, typed something, and then turned the laptop around to face her. 'Here's the sample format I've come up with for your website.'

On the screen was one of her well-known paintings, a depiction of children playing together in a sun-soaked field. The image was flushed to the left and shone against a white background. The painting's edges were soft, and the menu at the top of the screen repeated its colours. Working upside down at the keyboard, Dash reached around the side of the screen and selected the page, "About the Artist." There was a picture of Elena painting in her old garage studio in London. Alongside was dummy text in dark grey. Dash chose the next page from the menu, which featured her paintings, and even a few of her ceramics and bronze work, which had not been widely sold. There seemed to be a compliment in his choosing those works, and it made her happy to think he considered those as worthy as her paintings. But perhaps she was reading too much into it.

Dash broke her reverie. 'The other pages for the contact and so forth are blank at the moment.' He waited for her response.

She felt as though she could be honest and he would simply take it as direction, not as an insult to his design. His self-assured manner made him even more enticing, the way confidence in a man will do.

'I love it.'

'Really? I'm chuffed.'

'The picture of me…I'll have a new one taken. I'm pleased you've included all aspects of my work—the other mediums. I hadn't thought of doing that.' Her words were coming easier now. 'That shows my scope as an artist and perhaps reintroduces me to people who've only been to museum exhibits that show paintings. Which is lovely, because I want to continue working in those in future. And the page suggested by the menu, where it says, "Reaching Out." I was just thinking about the charities and people I hope to help support, and it's as though you already knew that. I'm amazed.'

He seemed pleased, but didn't comment on her evaluation. 'I'll have Samantha contact you, shall I? She's a writer who does excellent profile and human interest articles for the *Guardian* and other well-respected outlets. She's a bit pricey, but I'm convinced she'll be worth her fee.'

'Yes, perfect.'

He leaned slightly backwards in his chair, indicating their brief meeting was over.

She felt stunned, unable to just stand and walk away. 'I enjoyed seeing your work. Your sculpture, I mean. On your other website.'

'Thank you,' Dash said with a slow smile. 'That's quite a compliment, coming from an artist of your calibre.'

Silence continued for a few beats.

They stood, and she reached out to shake his hand. His palm engulfed hers and was warm. 'Thank you again. It was lovely to meet you.'

'My pleasure.'

She stayed two seconds longer than she should have, then turned and walked away. As she closed her vehicle door, she realised she hadn't tasted her coffee or even offered to pay him for it.

'Mum, maybe she expects you to ring.'

Charlotte knew she was annoying her mother, but she also believed Elena Dalca to be sincere when she'd agreed to meet Charlotte's family. 'Because it's your house, so she wouldn't necessarily ring up and say she's coming 'round even though I invited her.'

'Yes, you're probably right,' Bess Seabury agreed with her daughter. 'But I really don't have time, Charlotte.'

It wasn't any use. Charlotte grasped enjoyment when she could, but her mother seemed to habitually avoid it. Work was the only language she spoke. Since duty was the only call to which her mother responded, Charlotte changed her approach.

'It is a sacrifice, Mum, I know. But I'll help you when we get home. Because it's down to having good manners, you know. I *promised* Miss Dalca.' Charlotte allowed a frown to press her lips, showing her mother how much she, too, loathed any disruption in their mundane routine.

Bess let out a defeated sigh. Charlotte was correct. Social standards must be maintained, and now was as good a time as any to walk over to Bytheway, on the northern boundary of their farm.

'We'll just drop by and meet her, all right? I do hope she's home. Does she eat normal things?'

'Normal things?'

'I put up jars of my best soup yesterday, that batch of beef vegetable. Is she a vegan or other?

'I've no idea. We only talked about the library closing and Phoebe, then we went along to the shop where she bought pottery.'

'Regardless, I'd rather not go empty-handed. I shall bring her jam, the no-sugar-added. I've never known a person who objects to homemade jam.'

Charlotte knew it would be down to her to mind five-year-old Sarah on their little excursion to Bytheway. Her two middle brothers were playing football until five o'clock in the village, and her father would go and collect them. Her mum wouldn't want to stay at Elena's very long, lest she be late getting their dinner on. Charlotte wouldn't complain if they only stayed at

Elena's for five minutes. She often had the hollow feeling of always being on her own whilst living in a house full of people. This was a rare opportunity for Charlotte to spend time with her mum, doing something besides cleaning, cooking, and pegging out the washing.

Bess Seabury and her daughters walked down the lane, noticing signs of spring. Once on the road, little Sarah made a game of walking in a straight line, exactly where the grassy verge met the pavement. Charlotte and her mother were companionably lost in their own thoughts. In a few minutes, they turned and walked between the stone posts at Bytheway. Coming from the forest and out into the clearing, they heard piano music.

'That'll be coming from her studio, I reckon,' Bess said to her daughter.

Charlotte hesitated. 'Maybe we shouldn't bother her.'

'*Sans Peur,* Charlotte.' "Without fear," one of the Royal Air Force mottos that Bess had woven into her family's collective consciousness. Bess' father hadn't gone in for cringing and creeping about. One was to rise above, with strength and resolution. Bess had kept the faith and instilled the same principles into her family.

'Ms Dalca told you that she wanted to meet her neighbours, and here we are. Check your posture, and smile when you see her.'

'Yes, Mum.'

Charlotte agreed and mentally bucked up. Having confidence in yourself was underappreciated, especially by people in year 10 whose grandfather hadn't been in the RAF. But Charlotte had also learnt the hard way that people tended to laugh at her opinions. She'd coped with her share of name-calling. No one had been nasty towards Phoebe--or openly abusive towards Charlotte--when she had still lived in Marris Mynd. But Phoebe had been gone a long time now, and the two years

A.P. (After Phoebe) had not always been rosy. It was consoling to know that she had a new friend; a famous, beautiful, amazingly talented friend like Elena Dalca. And now they were going to see where she lived. Charlotte smiled at the thought.

In her most efficient mode, Charlotte's mum marched up to the studio, smoothed her ginger hair away from her freckled, pug-nosed face, and rapped on the door. They heard the music stop, then steps could be heard approaching the door. The suspense was terrible. Charlotte wore a toothy smile in advance so that she wouldn't forget.

Elena opened the door. There was a moment of processing. Then she said, 'Oh, Charlotte, you've brought along your mum. And who is this little petal?'

Charlotte relaxed. The smile had worked.

Bess' voice was animated. 'This is our youngest, Sarah. Sweetheart, say hello.'

Sarah put her fingers in her mouth. Bess swatted her hand away, but instantly gave up on making the child speak.

'Do you play the piano?' It was probably a daft question, but Charlotte felt she needed to assert herself (and please her mum) by saying something. Especially since the typically speechless Sarah had plugged her mouth and embarrassed her.

Elena smiled and tucked some of her long dark hair behind her ear. 'No, I don't. But sometimes I like to listen to Chopin whilst I paint. Do you play, Charlotte?'

'No.' Charlotte wanted to ask if Elena Dalca, the orphan turned famous artist, remembered her parents, who had died tragically. But, obviously, her mum actually didn't want her to talk, at least not yet, because at that moment, she rushed in and took over.

'Bess Seabury. We live just south of you, on the next farm.'

They were shaking hands. 'Elena Dalca. I meant to respond to Charlotte's invitation and introduce myself to you earlier this week.'

'I'm sure you're very busy.'

Charlotte noticed that her mum's lips were tightly drawn. It was odd to see one's mother slightly out of her depth—or something. Charlotte wasn't sure.

The conversation slammed to a halt.

Then Elena said, 'I've been living in one of the cottages. The larger one with a loft. Would you like to see it?'

Charlotte's mother said, 'Why, yes.' Which was strange, because they'd all seen the cottages a million times.

Charlotte followed Bess and held Sarah's hand as they walked down the alley--or

la ruelle Charlotte thought, French being one of her best subject --and crossed the lawn behind Elena. They filed into Elena's cottage. Charlotte wished she could live next door in the other one. She would have her own room instead of sharing with Sarah.

'Oh, you've made it so welcoming,' Bess exclaimed. 'It hardly looks like the same place.' Her mum sounded a bit more normal.

'You've been here before?'

Here was her chance to speak up. 'Mum used to be the cleaner. When the Smiths were here.'

'Yes, that's true,' her mum confirmed. 'They were lovely. But quite a bit more formal in their tastes, which is why the cottage looks so changed.'

Elena said, 'I'm glad that you like it. And I suppose I had that impression of the Smiths already, with the decorating in the house. Lots of old wallpaper, isn't there?'

Bess nodded, again with the tight little grin on her face. Charlotte could see both women thought the wallpapers were ugly, but they weren't saying so. She was proud that her mum and Elena saw things eye-to-eye.

'Come through,' Elena said, going towards the narrow corridor towards the back, where Charlotte knew there was a bedroom with an en suite bath. It was a treat to be shown

Elena's private space. She knew from online that Elena had done loads of interviews and had her picture taken a lot, but Charlotte would bet a fiver that none of those reporters and artsy people had been invited into Elena's home like this. They weren't mates with her, like Charlotte.

There was a sort of rug thing hanging on the wall done in reds, oranges, and blue, which made Sarah point and giggle. It was sort of like a bunch of intersecting triangles. Charlotte didn't know what style it was (or, indeed, if it had been made to go on a wall in the first place), but she felt that Elena had made the cottage very cosy, with lots of cheery colours. Their furniture at home was done up "in dark colours that didn't show the dirt." Charlotte liked their own house a bit less. Decorating solely for stain prevention didn't look as good as how Elena did things.

Mum and Elena were talking about the other close neighbours. Obviously, Mum didn't know that Charlotte had already covered this. Charlotte wandered away to look at some objects on the windowsill. She bent at the waist, her hands on her knees, to get a closer look at a small sculpture. It was very sweet; a little girl in a dress the colour of a buttercup. The little girl had closed eyes and wore a wide smile, with her face turned up, as though she was catching the warmth of the sun, and she sort of hugged herself at the waist. It was happiness.

'Do you like that, Charlotte?' Elena was talking to her.

'Yes,' Charlotte said, standing and turning. 'It looks like Sarah.' Bess and Sarah came closer to look at the small figure.

'It does,' Elena agreed. 'But Sarah is much prettier!'

Sarah smiled broadly and stuck her fingers in her mouth.

Mum forgot to correct her this time. Her mum was complimented. Sarah was as pretty as Charlotte was not.

Elena joined them at the window and said, 'It's yours if you would like it, Charlotte.'

'Really?'

'Oh, we couldn't accept,' Bess said. She looked extremely concerned. She'd forgotten that Charlotte and Elena were mates.

'No, I insist,' Elena said, laughing. 'It was one of my first attempts at ceramics. I'd forgotten I even had it until it came out of storage. Charlotte helped me choose some beautiful pottery the other day and didn't buy anything for herself. So, she should have this.'

Charlotte didn't have to be asked twice. She picked up the figurine. It was lovely. She crouched down. 'Do you want to hold her, Sarah? Be gentle.'

Sarah was taken with the ceramic and looked up at their mum, beaming.

A few moments later, Bess gifted Elena with the jam. Charlotte thought it was a little odd when Elena said, 'No one has ever given me anything like this before. Thank you so much.'

Charlotte decided Elena was fairly easy to get on with if she was *that* excited about jam. It was probably one of the things she liked best about Elena--rather than how Phoebe had always expected only the most expensive, store-bought-version of everything. Charlotte would carefully compose a proper note of thanks for the ceramic figurine as soon as they returned home. And hopefully, she would get the chance to tell Mum during the walk home that she'd remembered her thank you note responsibility without having been reminded. Mum was very big on always telling Charlotte what Charlotte already knew.

CHAPTER 14

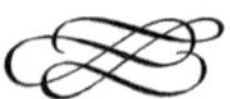

Another week had passed. March melted into April and green shoots popped up from the soil all over Elena's property. At the end of a long day of work, Elena stood on the lawn behind her large, locked-up house, staring out over an amazing view. The sun was setting over the hills, their craggy tops browned like toasted peaks of meringue. Beneath, the hills were speared with tall emerald green trees. Her tummy rumbled. She had forgotten to eat again. The sky was morphing into shades of peach now. A peach tart would be heavenly. There was nothing in the larder, save a jar of homemade jam from Bess Seabury, but it seemed too much of an effort to think of what to buy and then driving somewhere to get it.

She turned away from the majestic sunset and wandered towards her cottage. Everything she'd wanted had happened. She had all of the time in the world to paint. A perfect studio where no one would interrupt her, except the occasional delivery or neighbour dropping by. And she'd had no further harassment from her guardians since Roman had been warned off by Bryan Barker.

Her thoughts lingered on how life used to be. The heavy

work demands and extensive travel. A memory surfaced of being in Japan, waiting for a flight in an airport terminal and being completely overwhelmed with mind-numbing exhaustion. She had had the feeling that night that she simply couldn't go on.

That was all behind her now.

However, it wasn't quite that simple. Elena had always been surrounded; there were people hired to feed her, organise her schedule, and provide her essentials--everything from hair products and gourmet meals to pristine sets of luggage and new clothes to put in them. Roman had spoken with her daily about her work. They'd driven her hard, but in many respects, they'd created an environment in which she could thrive as an artist. And, if she were honest, she missed the structure they gave her life. She couldn't have imagined how draining it was just trying to figure out how to *live* day to day.

Adulting was difficult.

She remembered how desperate she had been to escape. But lately, she'd taken to listening to radio programmes in the evening in order to hear other people's voices.

Elena went into her kitchen for a cup of tea. The range was shut off in the big house now that everything was up and running in her cottage. She hadn't worked out where to get wood for the wood burner. It hadn't mattered too much, because there was a narrow, little "Everhot" Aga cooker. Its electric heat provided a little warmth and a homely atmosphere. Not comfortable, but sufficient.

She made the tea and looked at her phone. There was a missed call from her solicitor in London. Trepidation rose in her empty tummy as she listened to the message.

'Elena, Tobias DeBoer. Wanted to let you know I've filed legal action against Roman Giblin. An investments security officer rang to let me know of a fraudulent attempt by Giblin to access some of your funds. He submitted your personal information to try to force

entrance, but since you recently changed the passwords, it resulted in an alert. Security were then able to track his online movements rather easily. If you have any questions, ring me; otherwise, I'll keep you informed.'

Elena frowned. Roman's attempt at stealing should've upset her. He had already made millions from her; that should be enough. But she felt nothing. Roman, finances, and solicitors talking about serious issues seemed like another world, one belonging to London and the person she used to be. The room grew darker. Sunset had swept away, and dusk had slipped like a thief into the cottage. She carried her tea into her bedroom and stood it on the small table beside her bed. She undressed and slipped beneath the covers. She would drink her tea and read her book and sleep.

ELENA WOKE to heavy rain streaking down the cottage windows behind the thin curtains in her bedroom. Hunger drove her out from beneath the covers into an agonisingly cold room. She sped through a quick, mercifully hot shower and into a warm jumper and jeans. The nearest greengrocers were beyond her own village of Marris Mynd, down the road seven minutes or so, in Pulverbridge. Remembering the coffee shop where she had met Dash, she thought of stopping there first for a cup of coffee and a nibble. Then she could do the shop without feeling light-headed.

The short jog from her cottage to her vehicle soaked her hair and shoulders. She drove slowly down the hillside, around the bend, and into the village of Marris Mynd. Although it was early Saturday morning, she saw lights in the old library. There was a new message on the library's sign, but it was running with water and the angle made it difficult to read as she drove by. Passing the library, she drove on between the high hedges south towards Pulverbridge.

She thought of Dash Minton. A pang of humiliation needled her chest. He obviously wasn't interested in her as a person, as he'd sent only brief, professional emails to conclude the business of putting together her website. He lived rather close to Pulverbridge. She knew this because she'd noticed his address when looking at his website, and she had looked it up on a virtual map. His home wasn't pictured because apparently it was deeply nestled in a stand of large evergreen trees. She wondered about what sort of house Dash lived in. It occurred to her that maybe he didn't live alone. Perhaps with a partner, or even a wife and children.

She drove past the coffee shop.

Dash had created a wonderful website for her, representing her simply as a young artist who loved her craft and was striving to put her best work forward. The writer had written a biography that was factual but not glowing, which was exactly the approach Elena had wanted. Roman's approach had been to gather over-the-top "quotes"--gushing praise from celebrities, museum directors, and universities, with mortifying phrases like, "Dalca is a visionary of passion put to paint; a relevant artist for our times." One reviewer laid it on particularly thick, writing an essay describing her work as, "perspicacious postmodernism shouldering accents defying aesthetic semantics."

Elena hadn't a clue what that even meant.

Within a quarter mile, she came to the village centre. She turned by a red and black petrol station and made her way into a spacious car park in front of the supermarket. There was a little bakery alongside a beauty salon, and so she stomped her way through the rapidly deepening puddles to reach it. Elena pulled open the fogged glass door and stepped in, instantly overwhelmed with the luscious smell of fresh bread.

The place appeared to be empty. She walked up to the counter, her stomach churning in hunger. Scanning the menu, she decided what she would order, if, in fact, anyone was coming from the back of the shop.

She cleared her throat. Nothing.

She felt rain making its way from her soaked hair down the back of her neck. She shivered and wondered again how it was she had never had any rain gear in London, so had nothing to bring with her to Shropshire.

Another minute passed. Just as Elena was about to give up and leave, a woman in an apron, peeling off quilted oven gloves, burst in from the back.

'Hello,' she said. 'So sorry, love. I called out but you probably couldn't hear me, and I had to finish putting the buns in or I'll have nothing at ten when they all come in. Now, what shall I get for you, miss?'

Elena felt self-conscious. She could think of no witty banter with which to reply, and so she ordered a sausage roll and coffee. Then the kind baker gave her the coffee free to apologise for the long wait, and she kept right on chatting about all the lovely things she was baking. Elena couldn't have gotten a word in, but the baker's prattling helped her feel a bit less clumsy. She smiled enthusiastically, paid silently, and left.

Then she was back out into the rain, getting freshly soaked with torrential rain. She crossed the car park into the supermarket. Pushing her trolley, she took a desperate sip of the coffee and burnt her tongue. Elena stepped into an aisle lined with baking supplies and set the coffee down carefully on the child's seat. She felt as though she'd never been in a supermarket in her life. On second thought, when *was* the last time she'd been in a supermarket? Feeling self-conscious but famished, she reached for the sausage roll and took a bite. It was divine. She gobbled it down, standing alone by the flour, and by then the coffee was the perfect temperature.

Perhaps because of the bucketing rain, the store was virtually empty. She wandered, finding treasures. Shopping was fail-proof, since she had no food or provisions in her cottage whatsoever, with the exception of three teabags and the half-empty toiletries brought from the bed and breakfast. The big house had a huge utility room with a washer and dryer, but she hadn't any washing powder, so she added it to her purchases and carried on to the next aisle.

An hour later, Elena's trolley was full and weighed a tonne. She'd gathered some food to stock her pantry, but most other items were wants, including books, an intriguing packet of recycled wood "heat logs" for the wood-burner, saucepans, and a beautiful orchid in a swirly green and white pot. She paid for it all and sheepishly accepted help to heave her purchases into the back of her vehicle.

Driving into Marris Mynd, curiosity got the best of her. She pulled off the high street and into a space alongside the old library. From here she could properly read the sign: *New! Marris Mynd Saturday Market. Nine till Noon.*

Elena stepped out of her vehicle and felt chilled from the damp clothing hanging on her shoulders. Whether or not they would have any items of interest was irrelevant; she had longed to go inside the beautiful old library since the moment she first saw it.

Opening the heavy door with its ancient wrought-iron hardware, she wasn't disappointed. There was indeed a bit of fairy dust in the air. The ceilings were stupendously high, large oak tables were set up in rows, and the building bustled with people. She looked for a familiar face, hoping to see one of the few people she knew. None were there.

A petite young woman, perhaps Elena's age, was suddenly at her side.

'Hello, and welcome to our first-ever market day.' The girl had a gentle way of speaking and long blonde hair that shone. Her face radiated goodwill, putting Elena immediately at ease.

'Thank you.'

'I don't believe we've met. I'm Willa Purslow.' The girl extended her hand, which felt warm in Elena's clammy fingers.

'How do you do? I think we're neighbours,' Elena said, hoping she remembered correctly.

'Oh? Then you must be the artist, Elena Dalca?'

Elena nodded.

'You're quite right,' Willa Purslow said. 'We're your neighbours on the opposite side of the road, at the top of the hill. Come, meet my sister and her husband.'

Elena followed Willa to a table full of beautifully arranged seasonal produce, including a basket full of purple greenhouse-grown artichokes that were worthy of painting. Behind the table was a handsome couple. Willa's sister, Mollie, looked nothing like Willa; she was as tall and reedy as a fashion model with long, dark auburn hair. Elena was told that Mollie's husband had grown all of the produce on both the tables before her, and his name was Rhys. Rhys had a friendly handshake and a strong build. Her thoughts flew again to Dash Minton.

After meeting Willa's family and buying some vegetables from Willa's brother-in-law and goat's cheese from Mollie, Elena visited the other tables in the library. One was occupied by an elderly couple. He was thin and stooped and wore a pleasant expression beneath his wavy white hair, and the lady standing next to him had rosy cheeks and wore a knitted lavender hat and matching gilet.

'Hello, love, nice to see you,' said the lady. 'I do a bit of knitting, you see. Keeps me busy.'

'Keeps me busy too,' said the elderly gentleman. 'I put my hands out this way'—his palms faced each other—'and then she can spiral the yarn into a kitten's ball.' He turned to look at the old woman as though she were the most beguiling female to think of such clever things.

There was a stack of carefully folded throws.

'They're beautiful,' Elena said, running her fingertips over the perfectly defined cables in the heavy yarn.

'Now, those are right for when you're watching telly,' the lady said with a generous smile.

'I'd like a green one, please.'

'Oh, right! How lovely!' The woman clapped her hands and laughed. 'Did you hear that, Mr Ballard, the young lady is going to purchase our wares. Sorry, love, I'm a bit fired up because you're our first customer!'

'I've got a special carrier bag for that, miss,' said the gentleman, slowly reaching beneath the table. He brought back up a paper bag and was proud to offer Elena such excellent service.

They took her money and fussed and twittered and sent Elena on her way with a matching green hat at no charge, 'For being our first, you know.'

Elena was grinning along with them as she turned to leave. As she walked past the Purslow family, Willa gestured to her to come close.

'Newly-weds.' Willa flashed her eyes towards the elderly couple, still fizzing to one another about what great fun it was to sell crafts.

'Seriously?'

Willa laughed. 'Old Mr Ballard and the Widow Crook used to accidentally meet here every Tuesday morning when it was the village library. After the place closed and they'd been "meeting" for seventeen years, they decided to kick things up a notch. They had the reception here at the library, of course, almost a year ago, last spring.'

'That's the sweetest thing I've ever heard.' Elena shared a parting smile with Willa, then walked out of the library feeling much better than when she'd driven by less than two hours ago.

CHAPTER 15

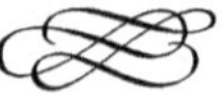

Oliver had endured his oral exam and submitted his final papers.

'I'm so happy for you, Oliver. I knew your presentation would be a success. You've worked so hard.'

'I feel like such a weight has lifted. I almost can't believe I'm finished at university.'

Willa looked at her lap and admired her blue dress. She had waited for just the right occasion to wear it, and this evening was perfect. Oliver was home for two days, and they were having dinner with his parents at a posh restaurant.

The dress had been a surprise gift from her sister. For the last two years, Mollie had travelled twice monthly by train to Birmingham, where she stepped out of her role as a goat farmer and artisan cheese maker and became a fashion model. It was a rather unlikely part-time job for a woman who'd grown up stomping around the farm in her father's passed-down clothing, but, as Mollie said, the money was too good to pass up. So, Mollie routinely peeled her tall frame in and out of a half-dozen outfits and walked in rotation with other models to put on luncheon or dinner shows for whatever fundraising event or social happening was in progress.

Recently, Mollie had done her first trunk show for an up-and-coming London designer. It was then that she'd had the opportunity to buy a dress from last season for her petite, blonde sister at a deep discount.

'But it's not my birthday or anything, Mols!' Willa had said, already pulling off her clothes to try the dress on.

'And I'll owe you forever for mucking out my goats, Wills!' Mollie had replied.

Willa had purchased a pair of shoes in a dark pewter shade that set off to perfection the small rhinestone design that ringed the dress's neckline. She'd found a crushed velvet grey purse that harmonised with the shoes on a table at the market in Ludlow, where their mother, Lisa, lived with her husband, Sam.

'You look perfect,' Mollie had said as she'd stuck the final hairpin in Willa's hair. Mollie had learned a few simple up-dos during her modelling work. She'd also helped Willa apply eyeshadow and chose a glamorous colour for her lips. Willa took a photo of her and Mollie to remember the special sisterly moment. It would help the next time they had a difference in opinion, which could happen before Willa managed to leave the house.

Minutes later, Oliver and Willa were speeding away in Oliver's car. Oliver turned the conversation to her.

'Rhys opened up the library for the first time,' Willa told him. 'Remember I told you he had an idea to use it as a farmer's market on Saturday?'

'Did anyone stop?'

'Actually, he did an impressive amount of trade. Several people who'd seen his advert came to discuss business with him. Mollie signed on another grocer, in Oswestry, who wants to offer her cheeses.'

'They must have been delighted with the response.'

'Definitely. And our new neighbour came, so we were able to meet her.'

'I've forgotten you have one. Remind me.'

'D'you know, I'm not sure I mentioned her to you. She's a famous artist called Elena Dalca. She bought Bytheway from the Smiths.'

'Wearing a beret and a smock?'

Willa laughed. 'No. Very pretty and young, and you'd never know she's such a well-known person. She was soaking wet, actually. It poured with rain as she was coming into the farmer's market.'

'Ah, what a nice welcome.'

'Elena was very sweet, despite dripping on the floor. Oh, and you may be happy to hear that I've had a change in my perspective.'

'How did that come about?' Oliver turned and glanced at her.

'The way a lot of my epiphanies do; I've been to see Granny. She helped me understand...better. And I spoke to Rhys. He had some good suggestions too.'

'So, you've had some new inspiration about our future?' Oliver asked.

Willa laughed. 'I still don't know what I want to do. But I know that I love you.'

'I love you too,' Oliver said, reaching out his hand to hold Willa's. 'And I promise, now that I'm home, we'll have all sorts of major discussions, about anything you like.'

'As long as we can do so *peacefully,*' Willa replied.

Oliver shot a glance at her to confirm that he had the same desire. His parents' recent row had left everyone around them very thoughtful, with a new enthusiasm for sorting out problems before they reached a boiling point. 'I daresay we won't see the likes of that sort of dispute again. And, I'm happy to report, they seem the better for it. I think they cleared out more cobwebs than what we all imagined. They've probably found a new direction for both work and how they get on.'

'I'm happy for them. And for us,' Willa said, very much in love with her fiancé and not caring a jot about work.

'I'm afraid it's me that he's got it in for now.'

'What?' Willa said.

Oliver wore a stern look on his face. 'I'm hoping it will pass and I'm planning not to antagonise him at dinner.'

'What are you talking about?'

'We can discuss it more later.'

THEY ENTERED the restaurant and were shown to the table already occupied by Oliver's parents.

'Hello, darling girl.' Oliver's father was on his feet as soon as he saw them approaching. He lightly held Willa's shoulders and brushed her cheek with a kiss. He shook hands with Oliver before the couple sat down. Lord Ranson signalled to the waiter and ordered a Scotch and water for his son.

'Willa?' he said.

'Just water with lemon, thank you.' Willa took Colleen's hand across the table and gave it a squeeze, and they complimented each other's dresses. Conversation was light while they received drinks and ordered their meals. Willa couldn't sense any tension between Oliver and his father, despite Oliver's cryptic comments in the car. She began to relax and enjoy the evening.

Willa was enthralled with the selections offered for the three-course meal. She lost the thread of the social goings-on whilst trying to figure out what seasonings were used in the artistic dots-of-sauce that punctuated the scallops, salsify, parsley, and smoked duck for the first course. As she savoured the last bite, she looked up to find the Corbett family smiling at her in silence.

'What? Oh, heavens, how embarrassing!' Willa covered her mouth with her hand.

They laughed and Oliver lightly hugged her. 'My chef fiancée appreciates good food, don't you, sweetie?'

Their plates were cleared. Oliver looked at his father and said, 'All right, Dad, please come to the point before Willa is served the next course. It'll save me having to catch her up on all she missed on the drive home.'

Willa gave him a warning look and a smile at the same time, and Oliver kissed the back of her hand. The second course arrived at that moment, and Willa resolved to pay more attention to her fellow diners than the lamb over wild rice with golden chanterelles and purple sprouting broccoli that was set before her. She didn't entirely succeed, thinking about whether she should suggest to Rhys that he check to see if there was a good market for upmarket mushrooms. She had heard somewhere that you could grow on mushrooms in discarded coffee grounds.

Oliver's father took a long drink and cleared his throat and the table turned their attention on him.

'I have some good news and some bad news to share with you,' Alex said, rubbing his hands together as if in anticipation. He pushed his half-eaten food away.

Willa noticed that Oliver exchanged a look with his mother. She smiled in a relaxed way, and she sensed a release of tension from Oliver.

'As you're both aware,' he began, focusing his eyes on Oliver and Willa, 'the current political changes have wrought an enormous effect on my personal business holdings. I'm happy to say that there was a satisfactory conclusion. I wouldn't say it was ideal, but it's good.'

'You're not losing Myndcroft Hall, then?' Oliver asked.

Willa hadn't realised that was a possibility. No wonder his parents' marriage had been under a strain.

'No,' Alex replied. 'But unfortunately for you, I'll be spending a lot more time at home.' Willa was a bit taken aback by this statement. She glanced at Oliver, who was impossible to read.

His father continued, 'I'm not sure if you knew, Willa, but our country has held their position as one of the world's top exporters, responsible for shipping above four hundred and seventy billion pounds worth of goods each year. My brother and I have been exporting electronics and machine tools for over twenty-five years and doing rather well out of it.'

Willa hadn't known how Lord Ranson made his money, and she'd never asked. It seemed rude to be inquisitive about their finances, and when she hadn't practised the same wariness with Colleen, it had brought a temporary rift between them. She did remember Oliver saying that his father had a "variety of business interests," and that had been enough for her.

Oliver's father explained, 'New trade agreements will be carried out under the World Trade Organisation rules, meaning we would incur a wide range of heavy taxes that make us much less competitive. Without knowing the long-term effects the new policies would carry, Thomas and I decided that if we could sell out and salvage some of our investments, then we would do so.' Lord Ranson paused and took a drink. He clasped his hands together. 'I'm happy to say that we got an excellent offer from a company in Belgium who owns another long-standing company in the UK. Best of all, they seemed keen on as little disruption of the business as possible, keeping on the same British workforce, since the profits were steady and everything's been ticking along smoothly for the last five years.'

'Congratulations,' Willa said, and received warm smiles from Oliver's mother, but for some reason, Alex looked away as though he hadn't heard her.

'That's wonderful, Dad. It sounds as though there are winners on every side.'

Alex agreed. 'Yes. Whilst the country works out what they

want to do, our company can carry on and be viable, with much less risk than having us in control.'

The waiter came and cleared the plates in readiness for the final course. Willa had selected a mouth-watering mix of dark chocolates and caramels stuffed with marmalade. She willed herself to find room for them.

'I gathered from what you'd said earlier that you've got another bit of news?' Oliver asked the question in a careful, diplomatic tone.

'Ah, yes,' Alex replied with a hearty laugh. 'Thomas and I got out of one mess and possibly into another, I'm afraid.'

Willa looked at Oliver's father for clarification. He didn't meet her eyes.

'We're finally doing it!' Alex laughed.

Then Willa watched in confusion as Oliver put his head in his hands. 'You're joking. How many years has it been?'

Alex turned to look at his future daughter-in-law. 'Willa, I've been threatening to develop a golf course in the region for donkey's years. It's finally a go. But for some reason, I've never been able to turn Oliver on to the game.'

'Because it's a never-ending bore,' Oliver said to Willa. He turned to his father. 'The acreage that you've had earmarked for the purpose?'

'Exactly. A few miles from Pulverbridge.' Alex turned to Willa, his eyes dancing. 'It is absolutely perfect for a course. The walking trails and pond are on the natural edge where the green will go, so there's little chance of upsetting the cyclists and tree huggers.' He smiled mischievously at Oliver, who biked the hills as often as he got the chance.

Oliver turned and smiled at Willa. They were both transported by the look that passed between them, and he scooted closer to her and put his arm around her.

She wondered what the changes in the family's fortune

would mean to her future. And what the underlying tension between Oliver and his father meant.

OLIVER WAS quiet on the way home. Another heavy rain shower had begun to fall, and loud drops assaulted the top of the small sports car.

'Is there something wrong?' Willa asked.

'No, sweetie. Everything's fine. Or, rather, everything's going to be fine.' Usually, a comment like that would cause him to smile at her reassuringly. He didn't look at her.

'Tell me now, what's happened between you and your father.'

Oliver sighed. 'We had a massive row.'

OLIVER THOUGHT back to the events of yesterday. He had been so surprised by his father's sudden change in mood. Instead of walking away, Oliver had carried on with his request, trying to bring his father around.

'I know the house hasn't been set up for weddings, Dad. But I'm not talking about a business strategy. This is my wedding. Mum always said we should be married from home. I don't understand the problem.'

Alex had exploded. *'It's still* my *house! You can do what you damn well please when you've inherited!'*

He couldn't remember having a worse argument with his father. And it had come when his parents had just patched things up. Not only had he managed to outrage his father, but his mother was disappointed that the carefully won peace had been shattered between them again.

. . .

Oliver ran his hand through his hair. 'I'm afraid there seems to be a change in our plans, Willa. My father doesn't want us to marry at the house.'

A peal of lightning sliced across the sky, illuminating Willa's stunned face, but Oliver wasn't looking at her. His eyes remained on the road.

She thought of all the plans she'd spent hours making, and all of the hard work she'd put in at the tearoom, trying to pay her share of the wedding expenses, despite Oliver's protests. Willa had wanted her family to be represented well, by her own efforts. Many of her added expenses were down to trying to match the grandeur of Myndcroft Hall. She said, 'He doesn't think I'm good enough for you. That's why. It's his way of washing his hands of me, publicly.'

'Willa! That's outrageous.'

She noted that he hadn't looked at her this time, either. And his voice lacked conviction.

They both were silent for the rest of the drive home.

Suddenly, her mind was made up. She was going to consult a professional for advice.

CHAPTER 16

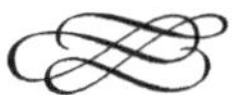

As Willa drove Rhys's truck into the village, she reflected on how much she'd changed in the last several years. Maybe change wasn't the right word, as she was fundamentally still the same person. She'd grown.

She had earned her cooking certificate, which had been challenging. Instead of Willa or Mollie moving out, it had been her mum leaving their farmhouse to marry Sam. Her younger sister, Phoebe, had left too, to live with Sam and Lisa at their home in Ludlow. Then Mum had a baby. And Mollie had married Rhys. Oliver had proposed.

A lot had happened.

All this added up and meant that she wasn't as nervous going to meet the vicar's wife as she'd been two-and-a-half years ago.

After speaking to Oliver, Willa had decided she needed help to sort things out. A different perspective. So, she'd phoned the vicarage.

'Veronica, remember when I came to have lunch with you and your niece, Katie?'

'When we lost you?'

'Yes.' Willa blushed even now. Veronica and Katie had gone

upstairs to look at Katie's new college clothes. Willa hadn't heard their invitation for her to join them, since she'd been in the loo when they called from the corridor. Then she'd been unable to locate them and had left the vicarage confused and upset.

'That was such a funny misunderstanding,' Willa said. She felt the mature attitude was to put it aside.

Veronica was laughing.

It wasn't that funny, Willa thought. As her sister had said often enough, Willa needed to learn to take herself lightly. She redirected Veronica's attention. 'I really valued your advice that day. As you probably know, I've completed my cookery course, just as you'd suggested.'

'Simply wonderful, Willa. Congratulations.'

'Thank you. I was wondering if I may be able to engage you, professionally, for another talk about my future.'

'Yes, and no,' Veronica had said. She'd agreed to see Willa, adding, 'I don't practice career counselling anymore, darling, now I'm a vicar's wife. So, you'll get my advice for free. How about that?'

Relieved, Willa had set an appointment with her for the following day.

Now, Willa arrived at two precisely, with a small book in hand for taking notes. The vicarage garden was alive with spring: camellia bushes in bloom, clusters of daffodils about to burst, and tinges of green were visible amongst the canes of Stephen's beloved rose bushes. Willa walked up to the gothic style door and knocked. Momentarily, she heard Veronica Hayward, her heels clicking against the flagstones in the hall, and the door opened.

'Willa!' she said, as though this were a random, fun surprise. Veronica stepped aside and then hugged Willa when she'd entered. Somehow, Veronica made everything exciting.

Veronica turned to the sitting room and welcomed Willa in.

Willa took a seat on the linen slipcovered sofa. Sitting on the low, dark wood table in front of her was a black toile tray bearing a tea service of red glazed pottery. 'I thought it might be cosy to have tea, but I couldn't summon the courage to bake anything for you. It wouldn't have been up to your standard. I begged a coffee cake from Mrs Jones.'

'What a treat,' Willa said. 'Hers are the best coffee cake I've ever had. Only she won't share the recipe!'

'Really?' Veronica, perched on a chair opposite to her, filled a large mug and handed it to Willa. 'I never had the nerve to ask. And now I never will. Not that it would do me any good. I'm an adequate cook, but hopeless at baking.'

Willa sipped the lapsang souchong but didn't care for its sophisticated, smoky flavour. She gladly accepted a slice of the coffee cake.

'I was at the tea shop last week, and Roni was singing your praises,' Veronica said, nibbling at a small piece of the cake. Willa marvelled at how Veronica had ended up here, in a small village, instead of doing something smart and glamorous in some vast metropolitan city.

'Roni has been very good to me,' Willa said of her boss. 'She's given me so much freedom to learn and to experiment with her menu. Which is one of the reasons I wanted to speak with you. I'm thinking about leaving there. I feel awful about it, leaving Roni short of help.'

'Mmm,' Veronica corrected her by humming, and swallowed her tea. 'No, Willa, you mustn't feel obligated to her. You've done her a good turn whilst you've been on staff. She confided in me--people always do, you know--that she's been well in the black since you've been there.'

Willa nodded. 'I suppose that's true. Even if I leave, Roni can carry on with those recipes if she chooses, and hopefully, keep making a good profit.'

'But at some point, Willa, the recipes will grow stale. Trends change, don't they? Even amongst goodies. I remember hearing about women who not only survived the recession, but became millionaires by opening cupcake shops.'

Willa agreed. 'Yes, you're right. It's amazing how quickly things change. Including pastries.'

'Have you considered working out an arrangement with Roni to function as her consultant?'

'What do you mean? Like supplying new menus and recipes later?'

'Exactly. You have a real flare, Willa. You're able to follow trends, but do it in a way that's familiar, so the local community isn't put off. If you were to decide on a fair price for coming in periodically and freshening her menu, I think she'd go for it.'

'That's a wonderful idea, Veronica! I'd never thought of it. I've had lots of ideas for Mollie's cheeses and goat products in the past, but she hasn't been open to them, so I guess I've not been thinking about contributing in that way since.'

Veronica smiled. 'Mollie's not the only person with goats, darling. And if you show her how someone else made a profit first, she'd be more likely to copy the model. Have you had any recent ideas?'

Willa blushed. 'Well, yes. At the moment, people seem to want low sugar, super healthful items. Yoghurt is moving from being artificially coloured and having sugar equal to a candy bar to a more healthful product. I think goat's milk yoghurt has a market amongst people who love a natural, farm-fresh provenance and want less sugar. Maybe also for those with allergies to cow's milk.'

'I think that's brilliant.' Veronica cooed, leaving Willa feeling empowered. She could imagine working on the process, developing a yoghurt recipe, and seeing the product in recycle-friendly packaging.

'These are exactly the sort of ideas I'd hoped to discuss with you,' Willa confessed. 'My mum is so, well, baby-brained at the moment, and my sister and her husband are excited about their own ideas for farming. They're not really keen to have me in the middle, if you see what I mean. Oliver, hasn't seemed to be able to think beyond finishing university--which, now that he has, he wants time off--and the wedding. Which I can completely understand...' Willa's voice fell off and she took another bite of cake.

'Would you like to hear the idea that I've been simmering in my thoughts for nearly a month?' Veronica's eyes danced. 'You see, I'd actually been biding my time, wondering how I ought to approach you. Stephen cautions me not to meddle too much, you know. It's so boring, not being able to tell people what to do.'

Willa set down her cake in anticipation. She was so sure that Veronica's idea would be wonderful that she picked up her notepad and pencil. 'Yes, please!' Veronica was such fun, Willa felt like she was spending time with a crazy aunt.

'Are you ready?' Veronica held up her hands dramatically. 'Here's the idea: I think you ought to make arrangements with Elena Dalca to lease her property. Or buy it. Whatever Oliver thinks.'

Willa was astonished. The notepad fell with her hands into her lap. 'Why?'

'Darling, don't you see?' Veronica's hands went flat on her thighs and she leaned over the low table and locked eyes with Willa. 'You could run it as a bed and breakfast. Of course, it needs doing up--it looks as tired as the Smiths were of having it--and I don't know if Oliver would care to live in or supervise from off-site. But if so, Myndcroft Hall is less than three miles from the Smiths' old place. But naturally, you realise that since you live across the road.'

A bed and breakfast? It seemed to Willa that she already was stuck making endless fry-ups for her sister and Rhys. She knew nothing about running a bed and breakfast and would rather muck out her sister's goats than to clear a stranger's hair from the bath drain.

'Oh, Willa, don't despair.' Veronica laughed.

Willa hadn't meant to show her disappointment. 'I'm sorry. But I just can't see myself…or Oliver…' Actually, she had no idea what Oliver would think of an idea like that. He was generally very at ease with people, but having them as houseguests might be another matter.

Veronica was undaunted. 'No apologies. We're just here to brainstorm, isn't that right? As for the other ideas, consulting at the tea room, and food product development ideas for something like the goat's milk yoghurt are perfect. So, we've already got some interesting projects for you to do, aside from being Mrs Corbett.'

Giggling, Willa agreed. But the giggle came from being called Mrs Corbett for the first time. She was so deliriously happy about getting married in two months that she couldn't think why she'd been so stressed these past weeks. Maybe things were just fine the way they were. She had been silly to be so upset, pressing Oliver to map out their lives in detail. Perhaps it was just wedding nerves manifesting in an odd way.

Veronica smiled patiently. 'I imagine that you and Oliver will probably want to begin a family sooner rather than later.'

'Yes, I'm quite keen on babies, especially since Mum and Sam have had little Elliot. Oliver is fond of him too.'

'But your mother is still working?'

'Yes, she is. I was sort of surprised when she wanted to continue. She's a very low-key sort of person, and before my dad passed away, she took her time finishing university courses. Then she got her position of heading up the library out of necessity of raising us on her own. You're right. I see what you're alluding to, though. And if I'm honest, I agree. I'll really thrive if I have something else to do beyond my home and motherhood.'

Veronica refreshed her own mug. She raised her eyebrows at Willa, but Willa declined more tea. Now that it was slightly cold, the tea tasted even more like an ashtray.

'Well,' Veronica said, 'the bed and breakfast is an idea I imagined may work for everyone. And I could, of course, be wrong, but I'm going to share my observations with you. If you'll indulge me?'

Willa had so much respect for Veronica's intuition that she couldn't help but be intrigued. 'Yes, please do. I didn't mean to dismiss the idea out of hand.'

Veronica took a sip of tea and studied the cocoa-coloured drape above Willa's head for a moment, sorting her thoughts. 'I think I'd be correct in saying that Elena Dalca wanted her property solely for the art studio. The price may have seemed exorbitant to us, but not so to a wealthy young lady with a guideline of London prices.'

Willa was stunned. 'You've been out to visit her at Bytheway? And she isn't very taken with the house?'

'Oh, yes. The house is shut up. Elena lives in one of the cottages and works in the studio. It seems no exaggeration to say that if the studio could be moved over by her cottage, then she wouldn't care who was coming up and down the drive!'

'I'm so surprised to hear that,' Willa said, thinking of her Granny Phoebe, who had lived for many years in a large house by herself. 'But what you're saying certainly adds up, because why would a single young person like her need a house of that size?' Willa pictured Elena and felt certain she must be lonely. Whatever the outcome of this discussion, she'd ask Elena to come across the road for dinner soon.

Veronica continued, 'I think Elena would be open to something being done with the house, so long as she could work without interruption. As far as a big-picture perspective, I think that the farmer's market idea of Rhys's will grow. And Alex is building a golf course in Pulverbridge.'

Again, Willa was surprised. She didn't think that Veronica was chatty with Lady Ranson, and Willa had only just found out about the plan for the golf course. It was odd how easily Veronica had assembled information from every direction.

Willa replied, 'So, if I understand what you're saying, the area around the village is becoming a bit more interesting. With a new golf course and more retail, a bed and breakfast would help tourism, overall?'

'Absolutely. Between us, I think Myndcroft Hall could earn its way hosting weddings and such. But, forgive me if I'm overstepping, that isn't to Colleen's current way of thinking at all. Oliver would be the person to make that happen.'

Willa's mouth opened slightly in shock. 'Oh.'

She couldn't possibly know anything about that *issue. Could she?*

Willa pushed the thoughts away, terrified that she may get teary since she and Oliver wouldn't be getting married at his family's country home.

Veronica gave her a dazzling smile and a scheming look. 'It's fun, planning things, isn't it?'

Willa smiled slightly, her head spinning with new information. Without really meaning to, she picked up her tea and drained it.

CHAPTER 17

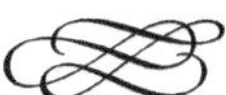

Upon her determination to have contact with other members of humanity at least once a week, Elena ventured into the village. It was then that she had seen the announcement for the art fair.

Today was Wednesday and she hadn't been from home since the previous Saturday. She returned to the chemist's with the nice shopping selections. The last time she'd stopped in, Mrs Andrews had greeted her young friend, Charlotte Seabury, and Charlotte had introduced them. Elena thought Mrs Andrews was very kind, and the sort of experienced pharmacist who'd know exactly what to do if you needed something health-wise. She had opened the shop some twenty years previously, and she seemed to be a sort of mum to the whole village, as well as professionally confidential and efficient. It was reassuring to know that Mrs Andrews was nearby.

Elena was about to step into the chemist shop when a brown-inked flyer caught her eye. The Shrewsbury Museum and Art Gallery were hosting a programme featuring a stained-glass artist, a talk by an expert on Victorian puppets, and a mixed-media exhibit by a local artist, Dashiell Minton.

Dash! Elena studied the paper intently. The programme began this Friday, with a special artist's reception on Friday evening. Tickets could be purchased for £20 and included "Welcome fizz and canapés, music from Shrewsbury School, an opportunity to explore the museum and art gallery, a licensed bar, and a silent auction." It was all to benefit the hospital League of Friends.

Coming into the shop, she was greeted by Mrs Andrews, looking slim and crisp in a white shirt that contrasted against her tan skin and short grey hair. She was changing her window display to a new range of spring items in Easter colours.

She stood on a small step, arranging plates on a decorative white dresser with slatted shelves that stood up in the window display area. 'Hello, Elena. How are you?'

'Mrs Andrews. Those are very pretty.'

'Sally, please. Yes, I rather like these plates. Especially the white with the pastel blue edging. You wouldn't believe the clobber I have at home. I just can't resist buying my own merchandise.'

'I'm glad to know you enjoy what you sell, though.'

'I can assure you that I do. Anything I can help you with today?'

'No. I really just needed to get out. I've enjoyed the pottery I bought with Charlotte. I don't suppose you still have the matching tray?'

'I have one left, actually. It's been moved over here; let me get it for you. Your timing couldn't be better, as this is twenty-five per cent less.'

'Perfect, thank you.'

'Elena, I couldn't help but notice from my window perch that you were looking at the flyer for the Shrewsbury Museum.'

'Yes, it's quite interesting. I'm thinking of going.'

'My husband and I will be driving down. Why don't you join

us? We'll be fashionably late because I'll need to close up the shop, but only by a half-hour or so.'

'That would be wonderful.' Elena felt somewhat guilty about accepting the invitation. She had been so dependent on Roman and his wife, and here she was latching on to another couple. She hesitated. 'Are you certain your husband won't mind? Isn't it a special evening out for you?'

Sally chuckled. 'No, we prefer a good meal if we do anything special. I'm afraid the catering for this event requires one to eat a light supper before coming. It's more along the lines of Tom being on the board for raising hospital funds, so we need to make an appearance. Your presence would help us jolly through the evening.' She smiled warmly and Elena felt it was okay to accept. Surely, attending a public event with new friends hardly made her a clinging nuisance.

'I would love to join you. Shall I meet you here at the shop before you close?'

'Yes,' Sally said whilst wrapping up her tray so that it wouldn't be chipped on the way home. 'I'll change in the back, and then Tom should be here.'

Elena hadn't thought of needing the proper attire. 'Oh, dear. I need something smart to wear.'

'Have you been clothes shopping since you've moved here?' Sally asked. 'Because there's a lovely shop in Church Stretton that is very chic. They even carry items from Italy. But in case you don't find anything to your taste, I'll write down the name of a shop in Ludlow, too.'

'Thank you,' Elena said. She paid for her purchase and said goodbye.

As she was this far from home already, and only had two days to find something to wear for Friday evening, Elena drove directly to the dress shop in Church Stretton. It helped to know that she could hardly go wrong; she needed so many clothes. Rain gear and new jeans were also on the list.

Elena located the address after driving past it once. She made her way into the shop. It had a thick black carpet, a low ceiling, and a swanky gold and glass display case. An impeccably dressed, friendly woman stood behind the counter and stepped out instantly to greet her. The shop appeared to be otherwise empty.

'Welcome. How can I be of help?'

'Hello,' Elena said, feeling as though she may as well be wearing a bin liner, so out of place was she amongst the stylish clothes. There was definitely nothing casual here to help her everyday clothes shortage. 'I'm going to a do at an art museum and need something to wear.'

'Shrewsbury, by any chance?'

'Yes, as it happens. Are you going too?'

The saleswoman smiled and said, 'I'm going to Wales for the weekend with my boyfriend, but I'm sure it will be a lovely evening. We have a few things over here that may suit you. They're a bit younger, as you are.'

Elena noted the Italian labels, just as Sally had described. The colours were vibrant, and the skirt lengths were high. The problem was, although Elena painted in these colours, she'd never been keen on wearing them. Not to mention she'd feel self-conscious in the revealing designs.

'No?' the saleslady asked.

'Do you have anything a little more understated?'

'Why don't we look at these?' She walked with Elena to a corner where there were dresses marked at a discount. It seemed to be her lucky day to find a bargain.

'They're not new for spring, but it will be quite cold on Friday evening. You'd probably be glad of the sleeves and heavier material. Since it's not yet Easter, I think one of these would be suitable.'

Elena was immediately drawn to a heavy silk dress in

amethyst with a surplice bodice that gathered at the left side. 'I quite like this.'

'That would be gorgeous on you, and they ran quite small, so we're sure to find one that fits nicely. Let me pull several for you to try.'

Elena stepped into a dressing room with a mirror that covered the entire back wall. As she zipped in, the saleslady shoved several boxes beneath the curtain. 'Personally, I think the dark emerald shoe is lovely with that dress, sort of a peacock combination of colours, you know? But we have these in black, too.'

'Thank you, I'll try a pair.' Elena found that she'd correctly guessed her shoe size. She slipped on a pair of heels, which seemed comfortable, considering. She looked at her appearance. The dress skimmed her figure. Its aubergine colour looked well with her dark hair and pale skin. The dark green court shoes were interesting and slightly edgy, without being brash. Elena was pleased and decided to purchase the beautiful dress and shoes. She casually found herself thinking that Nichola would approve her choice; for all of her cruelty, Nichola had chosen suitable and pretty things for Elena to wear over the years.

She redressed in her working clothes and came back out into the shop. Draped across the glass and gold counter was an evening wrap in the same amethyst colour as the dress, with an emerald lining that would peek out here and there. The helpful saleslady also chose some very sheer stockings, a small evening bag, and some delicate jewellery.

'You have wonderful taste,' Elena said, complimenting her choices. She felt grateful that the woman had thought of everything. 'I'll take all of it, please. And thank you so very much for your help.'

'Absolutely, miss, it was my pleasure,' the saleslady said. She obviously enjoyed employing her talent. Elena handed over her credit card.

The sales clerk said, 'I'm so sorry for any inconvenience, but we don't take this type of card. Is cash a problem?'

Elena happened to have quite a lot of money that she'd kept in her handbag, saved over from her days of trying not to leave a trail for Roman and Nichola to find her.

The saleswoman took her payment, and said, 'I hope you'll come again soon.'

RHYS AND MOLLIE were walking out to inspect the goat pasture. The goats could be rascals, so it was good to periodically inspect the grazing fields for weak areas in the fence that could facilitate escape or potential harm.

'Can I join you?' Willa asked.

'Yes,' Mollie answered. 'It's chilly and wet, though, not like yesterday. It's been so cold; I'm dying for summer.'

Willa went to the boot room to get a warm waterproof. The trio set off, their father's old dog, Tarrant, running excitedly ahead of them. His blue merle coat blended into the white and grey of the low-hanging clouds and drizzle.

They crossed the gravel drive that led up to the farmhouse, over the lawn, and then climbed over the fence to the pasture. Following Rhys to the left, they began a methodical stroll alongside the fence line.

'You had your meeting with Veronica Hayward?' Rhys asked. 'What had she to say, then?'

'It's rather shocking.'

Mollie tipped her head back and laughed. 'Do tell.'

Willa noticed that Mollie's mirth had caught Rhys' eye and his eyes shone with love for her. She hoped Oliver looked at her like that when she wasn't aware of him doing so.

'Her first idea was, I thought, inspired. She suggested that I offer to work as a sort of consultant and periodically update Roni's menu at the tearoom.'

'You'd charge a fee just for writing out the menu?' Mollie asked.

Her sister had a good head for business, even if she didn't always agree with Willa's more entrepreneurial leanings. 'I think for it to work, I would offer a whole programme. The menu ideas, the recipes, and maybe a trial run of the new food items so that Roni could sample everything. And perhaps working with the staff a bit, so they feel a level of comfort with the new dishes that they'd be making and serving.'

'Seems it'd pay off handsomely for Roni's business,' Rhys said. 'And be a nice earner for you.'

'But hardly shocking,' Mollie said. 'What else did she say?'

'I'm coming to it, but the next thing she said is that I ought to take my ideas for goat's milk to another producer.'

'Oh, I see. Someone with more vision than me.'

'Don't be offended, Mollie, please. If you want me to try to develop some yoghurt recipes, or anything we've talked about before, I'd love to give it a go.'

'I think you're ready to expand, love,' Rhys said, hugging Mollie about the shoulders as they walked.

'Really?'

Willa hadn't realised it before. All she had needed to bring Mollie on board with her new ideas was to talk to Rhys first. He was a risk-taker, and he gave Mollie confidence. Plus, there was the mere fact that she listened to him. If Rhys thought something was a good idea, Mollie's scope expanded to include it.

Rhys paused. He walked over to a fallen section of the pasture wall and began replacing the stones. Mollie turned to Willa and crossed her arms. 'Enough suspense.'

'Veronica suggested that Oliver and I run a bed and breakfast.'

'*What?*' Rhys and Mollie answered Willa's comment in unison.

'I know, that's what I thought. But I'm trying to be open-minded because, initially, I thought she was wrong about me earning my cookery certificate. And, yet, I've done it now, and I'm glad I did. She was right.'

Mollie wrinkled her nose. 'But what is Oliver meant to do?'

'She wasn't totally clear. And I wasn't very receptive.'

Rhys finished stacking the stones and they began to walk again. He seemed lost in thought, and Willa hoped he'd say something brilliant that would clarify things for her. He often did that.

They walked along in silence for a few minutes. Then Mollie said, 'You have a lot of energy and ideas, Willa. I could see you taking on a holiday let. But it's such a lot of hard slog and I don't see Oliver doing that at all.'

'Actually, Veronica shared something with me in confidence. Although, if you stop to think about it, anyone in the village could figure it out.'

'What's that?'

'Obviously, when the Smiths grew tired of Bytheway, which is the property she has in mind--'

'Isn't that where the artist girl is living?'

'Yes, Rhys. She owns the property,' Willa answered.

'That's a bit ridiculous.'

'Anyway, other people may have a role to play. Veronica called my attention to the fact that Bess Seabury has been out of a job for a long while, as the property didn't sell for ages after the Smiths went to France. The lack of income has been difficult for the Seabury family. I suppose that's one of the reasons that Charlotte is eager to help you with the milking when you need it, Mollie. Her earnings may have made a difference for them.'

Mollie sighed. 'I never thought about it.'

'What did Bess Seabury do over there?' Rhys wanted to know.

'She cleaned all of the guest accommodation. Seabury's

oldest boy kept the garden. There was another lady from Pulverbridge, Ffion Jones, who helped Bess clean and did most of the breakfast, while Mrs Smith saw to the guests and served the food.'

'So, you wouldn't have to do everything by yourself?' Mollie said. She was well aware that she couldn't have run her dairy without Willa, and then later, Rhys.

'Right. According to Veronica, Bess has taken some relief from the church. Not that we're meant to know, but in sharing that information, Veronica was putting me in the picture of how challenging it's been for them.' Willa paused and said, 'Rhys, what do you think?'

'I think it all hinges on the property owner's willingness, Willa.'

As usual, Rhys had got it in one.

CHAPTER 18

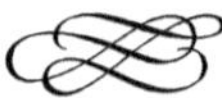

Elena met Sally and Tom Andrews as arranged, and they chatted like old friends as Tom drove them south to Shrewsbury. She was glad that she'd agreed to come along with them, and it hadn't been the least bit awkward. Tom Andrews was a councilman in the village and told her amusing stories about residents past and present. He was delighted to learn that she'd recently met the village newly-weds when she bought a knitted throw from Widow Crook, now the delighted Mrs Ballard.

'She was so excited when they came to the registry office that she wasn't sure which surname to sign on the marriage certificate, her old one or the new one,' Tom said, chuckling. 'They really are a pair.'

He drove into the town square and Elena saw the museum's neoclassical facade haloed in golden lights. Tom dropped her and Sally at the entrance, then drove off to find a parking spot.

'It's really beautiful,' Elena said.

'Yes, they do a number of weddings here.'

Weddings. What could be more fitting than for two artists to marry at an art museum? Embarrassed, Elena pushed the thought from her mind. Dash had only communicated with her regarding her website, and hadn't even made small talk with her, much less anything personal.

They were soon joined by Tom. 'We can view the art first, and then get drinks afterwards, if that's agreeable to you ladies.'

Elena followed the Andrews into the exhibit area. She looked without seeing the displays of stained glass and Victorian puppets. It seemed odd to be back in a museum but not taking part. Not to mention, she hadn't been in a crowd this size in a while, and felt slightly overwhelmed with so many people talking, stopping, and gently bumping into her as she followed the Andrews. They crossed a corridor and saw the sign for the main gallery: *Dashiell Minton, An Exploration of Wilderness Themes.*

Tom and Sally whispered to each other but didn't require her to speak, allowing her to carefully study the exhibit. Dash's finely wrought figures were impressive. The first, a graceful deer--life-sized--was fashioned from collected pieces of bleached wood. The setting included dried grasses and small evergreen trees. In another vignette, the artist had rendered a profile of the Shropshire Hills from burnished bronze. It hung suspended on a wall bathed in sunset-coloured lights that reflected off the metal.

And, perhaps her favourite, a most unexpected, delicate woodland fairy. The fairy's papier-mâché body wore a dress of textured bark and moss, with layers of light gold, gossamer silk hair. The energy of the onlookers around her was positive. The woman standing next to her said to her companion, 'Oh, look, Roger, how he's done that. How beautiful, and clever, too, don't you think?'

Dash's work had captured everyone's imagination, and Elena felt proud of him, even though she hadn't any right.

She stood alone by another bronze work depicting a fallen tree amongst a pillow of leaves when she had an odd sensation.

She turned to find Dash standing about a metre away. He was as handsome as ever in a black suit with a grey shirt and tie, hands in his pockets, gazing around the room and judging the reactions to his work. Few people in the room knew what Dashiell Minton looked like, and no one expected Elena Dalca to be there. They were anonymous. He turned to look at her.

'Elena.' He walked towards her, taking his hands from his pockets.

They shook hands as he leaned in to kiss her cheek. He smelled woodsy and just as delicious as he had in the coffee shop.

'Your show is magical.'

'Thank you.'

An elderly woman passed by, and with a high-pitched voice said to her friend, 'I'm sure this looks all right to some people. But you can't use these things, you know. Stained glass for windows and puppets for the children do make more sense to me, I'm afraid.'

Dash and Elena smirked. His demeanour was one of generosity and amusement. He stepped closer to Elena.

'Indulge me,' he said in a lowered voice. 'What was your favourite piece, and why?'

It was a question she'd often wanted to ask of people who viewed her work, particularly other artists. Not to seek compliments, but to gain something from another perspective, to share the experience of visual impressions and opinions about them.

'All of the pieces spoke to me, which is a rare treat,' she said to Dash. 'But the fairy, she was *unexpected.* She was in keeping with the theme of the woodland, yet she was of an entirely different inspiration. I wondered where she'd flown in from. And the brilliant addition of a little dry ice to clothe her in a mysterious mist as she was suspended above the forest floor... Even so, she somehow seemed more *real,* perhaps, than a fairy ought to be?'

Dash's face had been immovable whilst she was speaking. He frowned. 'Excuse me.'

Before Elena could ask him what was wrong or utter an apology, he was gone.

She stood for some moments in a daze. Presently, Sally and Tom circled back to her. Elena asked them what they'd thought of the exhibit.

'Definitely my favourite,' Tom said in a low voice to Elena and Sally. "Although that isn't much of a compliment given that we've seen badly copied church windows and creepy dolls.'

'Tom!' Sally scolded him, but she was laughing. 'I was enchanted with that deer. I could live with it very easily in our garden room, and then once in a while, I'd pop him in my front window at the shop as the centre of an amazing display.'

'Wouldn't that be lovely?' Elena decided to ask their opinion on the piece that apparently had just driven a wedge between herself and the artist. 'What did you think of the fairy?'

Tom said, 'She was a pretty thing, wasn't she?'

But Sally's brows went together and she looked the other direction without offering a comment.

What is she thinking?

Tom led them towards the balcony and the adjacent Walker Suite. Elena could smell savoury food and hear the chatter growing louder as they approached the mix and mingle area. She filed in the queue after the Andrews, and they collected hors d'oeuvre and wine. The beautiful balcony area had shining dark wood floors, and white columns against light grey walls which reached up to an ornate, domed ceiling. The balcony was lined with rows of round tables dressed in white linen, where they took their seats. Below, the Music Hall became alive with classical music. It was quite loud and Sally and Tom occasionally leaned in to hear one another's comments. A group of people sat down with them at the table. They were having an intense discussion about hospital funding, and diagnostic equipment seemed to be the focus.

Elena looked around casually, hoping to see Dash. Perhaps he'd had something else on his mind and really did need to immediately leave her. She knew better than anyone the behind-the-scenes stressors involved in having an exhibition of your work; the talks with sponsors, the interviews with local and wider-reaching press, the requests by the museum for live-event photographs with important attendees. Someone may have caught his eye that she hadn't seen, and he'd innocently assumed she'd understand his need for a quick departure.

But somehow, she didn't think so. She had managed to offend him.

She ate her food without enjoyment and found the wine too dry. The Bach melody ceased below. The Andrews turned about in their chairs, and she mimicked them, just as a man approaching a small stage came into view. The speaker welcomed everyone with the usual sort of script. He spoke about how this evening could positively impact the quality of healthcare for Shrewsbury and the surrounding areas, impressing upon the audience the need to be generous. Then the silent auction began.

It was Elena's first time attending an auction as a guest.

The auction began with some cruise holidays and Tom bet on one of these. He didn't win, but his bidding electrified the atmosphere at the table. The hospital people sitting with them seemed quite pleased, although none of them bid on anything. The auctioneer announced there were only six items remaining. His assistant then wheeled out a trolley which held a bronze statue of a graceful tree, an expansive canopy stretching out over the "grassy" base. Elena thought it was a breathtaking, beautifully rendered piece, with a familiar quality. The auctioneer then announced that the artist was "Dashiell Minton, whose work was exhibited here this evening."

The bidding began, and several people raised their paddles, causing the price to climb. As people noted and discussed the bidding amongst themselves, a hum of conversation began. Elena felt no rush of emotion, but she sat staring at the bronze. The art expressed a tree with an ancient, wise air about it. It had deep roots in a place where it had stood for decades, with limbs that provided shelter and peace. The landscape had changed around the tree, but the tree was secure. She liked that sense of security, the graceful lines of metal depicting branches that bent into the winds of change but didn't break.

She wanted it.

Elena barely heard the shush amongst the crowd as the auctioneer was about to award the tree to someone else. Her hand shot up. The other bidder, whoever it was, disappeared.

'Going once. Going twice. Sold to the young lady in the aubergine dress for seven thousand pounds.' Applause rippled through the venue.

SHE SAW Dash briefly at the close of the auction. They had a photograph taken together, each standing either side of the work that she'd purchased in the auction. He had thanked her most professionally. Then they left, and Sally and Tom made much of the whole thing in the car on the way home.

'I hadn't even realised you were paying any attention to the bidding,' Sally said. 'The next thing I knew, you'd made the biggest purchase of the evening. You're certainly full of surprises, Elena!'

Tom added, 'Yes, and no one dared look at me twice over letting a cruise go with the big spender at our table.'

She was glad that they were pleased since they had kindly allowed her to tag along.

No one had seemed to sense any tension between her and Dash. Maybe it had been her imagination.

CHAPTER 19

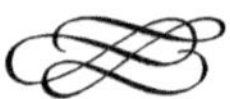

The nightmare caused his back and legs to straighten with the impact, waking him up. He sucked in his breath, and sat up in the tangled sheets, elbows on his knees, eyes still closed.

Unkindly, his memory began once more at the beginning of the sequence. He couldn't stop it, he couldn't open his eyes. For a few more seconds, he would sit in his bed, head in his hands, and unwillingly watch the story once more. It was a made-up story, shown in the theatre of his mind, and the story had lost some details over time and added others. He imagined he was in the car when his fiancée was killed. But he hadn't been; he hadn't even been in the same country.

His thoughts turned to parents. He ought to ring his mum; it had been a while since they'd spoken. A real memory surfaced, from his childhood. It was the only other time there had been a death of someone he knew, and somehow this memory had become entangled with *hers.*

His father was walking alongside him up to the small white house. Dash could feel his dad's large hand cupping the back of his small skull, pushing him along the walk to the front step. It was oppressively warm, and sweat made Dash's shirt stick to his back.

He'd tried to tell his father no, that he hadn't wanted to come here, that he didn't know what to say.

Then they were walking through the front door. Dash had expected to hear wails of grief from the two children and their father, but it hadn't been like that at all.

I'll speak to the gentleman, you'll minister to the children, his father had said.

Minister to the children? Dash hadn't a clue what that meant. His dad wanted to help everyone—like some vicar, only he wasn't. Dash's father did maths for companies, budgets, taxes, and things.

Dash tried to escape, but his feet wouldn't obey. His father, still pressing him forward, ferried him along into the kitchen. An expressionless man sat at the table. The man held a big blue plastic bag in his lap, the hospital's name printed across the front. He was silent. Just staring. At last, Dash's father released him and went to put a hand on the man's shoulder. Dash lingered for a moment, watching.

The man didn't respond to his father's touch. He just carried on staring out the window.

Dash turned and ran. He knew the man's children were in the front room, he'd seen them out of the corner of his eye. They sat together on the floor, Samuel, from his primary school, and his little sister. But what could he do for them? Their mum wasn't coming home. Ignoring them, he ran out the front door. He kept on running, past his father's car, down the lane. A few hours later, he was home and his dad punished him. But he didn't care if his dad gave him a smack.

Unravelling the sheets, Dash lay back down on his bed. He wasn't unsympathetic to other people's suffering. When his fiancée died, he'd gone to her parents' house. He'd hugged her weeping mother. She was so sorry for him, she'd said. Dash had said nothing and thought he ought to make her a drink. But as he'd stepped away, he saw a plastic bag by the sofa.

He knew it was full of *effects* belonging to the girl he loved. What a strange word for a dead person's things. Things no one wants to see, packaged up so that grieving people can smell the loved one they once held in their arms. Dash had turned and walked out her parents' front door.

No one had been angry at him for leaving or for taking so much time on his own after her funeral. His family had brought food and sat with him. The Sunday afternoon following her burial, they'd come around to do this. The kettle on, his parents sat side by side on the sofa. His mum had looked at her hands while his father gazed at nothing in the middle distance. This show of sympathy for Dash's loss had been a painful one, as his parents had never got on particularly well. It was commendable. They were trying to get past themselves and be there for him.

As the kettle had started hissing, Dash began laughing. Deep, snorting laughs. Holding his belly, unable to stop.

His mother and father had exchanged confused glances. The kettle had screeched and sang out as his parents sat, slightly horrified by his uncontrolled hilarity.

The chortles dissolved into tears, and he'd pointed at his father. '*You* don't know what to say.'

His father apparently hadn't remembered taking him 'round to see that family who'd lost the lady of the house. His parents didn't visit again. In fact, Dash mused as he got up from his bed, it had been the last time he'd seen his parents together. A few months later, his do-gooder dad had left his mother and moved to Cornwall to be with his girlfriend.

Everyone can master a grief but he that has it. Shakespeare had obviously known that other people are free to move on, even when you're not able. Dash realised that he just wanted his dad to be happy. And his mum. He'd never wanted them to carry on in misery. The thought caused him to take a deep breath and release something.

Walking into the bathroom, he looked at his face and dishevelled hair in the mirror. Oddly, a peaceful feeling settled over him. He felt new freedom from the past. The dream, he knew, wouldn't be back. There was an innate, inexplicable understanding that had come in the last few moments. He didn't know the why or how, but he knew it was good. He would get through cleaning his teeth, make a coffee, and ring his mum.

'AUNT LOUISE and the girls send their love too.'

'Okay, Mum, thank you.'

Despite his newish acceptance, Dash was relieved to end the call with his mother. They had had an adequate sort of relationship, but after his father had left her for another, much younger, woman, Dash's mother had become a grudging, vinegary version of herself. She identified with him not as her son, but as someone who mutually shared her loss.

He rang her up every month or so and made an appearance for her birthday and occasional holidays. Iris had been caught up in her latest misery—this time it had been her sister's bout with the flu, and as she and Aunt Louise lived together, his mum had disclosed disgusting details of every symptom. The sisters had three other friends of similar disposition, and the five of them moved in their own little world. His mother hadn't even realised that he'd been honoured with the exhibition in Shrewsbury, the town she now lived in, and he hadn't had the energy to interrupt her illness updates and village gossip to tell her. Besides, she would've only caught the fact that he'd been in town and not visited.

He may not be the most chipper of personalities, and he felt positively knackered after speaking with his mother. He decided to clear his head and take a run. Coal, his black Labrador puppy, began galloping in circles around the kitchen.

'How do you know? I haven't said a word.' Dash pulled on his trainers, grabbed Coal's lead in case he needed some restraint, and headed out of doors.

The spring chill was bracing. Coal ran towards the woodpile, nose to the grass, picking up some delicious scent. Dash whistled him up and they headed down the path, deeper into the wood that surrounded Dash's home. They heard the battle drill of a woodpecker trying to dislodge juicy insects from within the bark of a tree. Coal stopped below the tree and gave the bird a cursory bark, and then caught up. Coming around a bend, Dash hit the muddy part of the trail and sidestepped onto pine needles. The fragrance driving up from his pounding feet was like a sweet drug. Perspiration began to dew his skin, and the pup running out in front of him lagged a bit. Dash slowed to a walk, his hands coming to his hips as he caught his breath. Coal lay down, but in seconds, he was on his paws and brought a stick to Dash.

'Go!' Dash said, throwing the stick in the path of the dog. Coal gave a little hop and managed to stretch out his neck and catch it. Dash was impressed and laughed. 'Good boy.' They alternated between running and playing fetch on their return to the house.

LATER, after a hot shower, Dash dressed to go to the coffee shop for a good brew and to work on a new logo and website refresh for a client who owned a number of hair salons. Picking up his laptop and pulling the door behind him, Dash had just climbed into his vehicle when his phone rang.

'Dash Minton.'

'Mr Minton, it's Shannon from the hospital charity committee. Thank you, again, for allowing us to host your wonderful exhibit.'

'Entirely my pleasure. I hope the evening was a success for you.'

'It exceeded our expectations,' Shannon gushed.

Dash had enjoyed working with her and appreciated her advice about what sort of work to donate for the fundraising auction. She was thorough, efficient, and made sure that the museum staff gave him loads of support in setting up his exhibit.

'However,' Shannon continued, 'we've hit a bit of a snag, and I just wanted to let you know. We received a bad cheque for your wonderful donated piece. Since it was purchased at auction, we may return your art to you if the matter can't be promptly resolved.'

Elena Dalca had been the purchaser.

'No worries, Shannon. I hope, for the hospital's benefit, that payment will come through. If it doesn't, I'd be happy to come and pick it up. Unless you have another fundraiser coming up.'

Shannon laughed and said, 'I confess I was hoping you'd volunteer to allow us to hold the sculpture for the preceding bidder or another opportunity!' She explained that the hospital would participate in another county-wide fundraiser in June. 'Perhaps we'll be able to re-auction it at that time. I'll send you the paperwork, shall I?'

Dash agreed. They rang off.

He opened his computer and leaned it against the steering wheel. A quick glance at his accounts confirmed that Elena hadn't paid him for his work on her website. She seemed to be a bit clueless when it came to conducting business, but he had given her grace for being very young and having always had help. But they'd agreed that she would pay him when he'd finished her website design, and it was as straightforward as accounting could be. She was obviously careless and didn't realise that people needed money to live.

Enough with challenging women for one morning. He needed a coffee. Snapping his laptop shut, he threw it on the seat next to him and started the engine.

CHAPTER 20

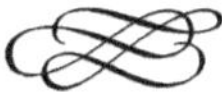

Elena put down her paintbrush and stepped back to view her work. The new painting was coming along nicely. She'd been painting whatever she wished without caring if it was what the public favoured or what her previous management would've wanted. Her instincts had led her to paint some of the freshest, most inspired work she'd done in a long time. Not that she hadn't always followed her heart, but she realised now that Roman had been constantly working her heartstrings to get certain results. Results that paid well.

Her mobile chimed. Her thoughts went immediately to Dash. She hoped that he would get in contact by phone or a brief message. He'd told her he'd be happy to respond to any questions about the new website he'd designed for her, but she hoped maybe he would follow up anyway. Either respond to her thoughts about the fairy he'd included in his show, or perhaps talk to her about her bid at the auction. Not that she had purchased the piece to obligate him to her—that wasn't at all the case. His art had struck a chord with her when she'd only just seen pictures of it on his website. It was almost inevitable that she would cherish a piece of his work through an acquisition.

As several days had passed since the auction, she became more convinced that she had deeply offended him. Worse, she didn't even understand how she had done it.

She walked over to a small cabinet that held her supplies and picked up her ringing mobile.

'Hello.'

'Settling in?'

She recognised her estate agent's voice. 'Bryan, lovely to hear from you. It is beginning to feel more like home, even though it's been less than a month.'

'Good to hear. I'm ringing to check in on you. Your website must be blowing up with visitors.'

'Sweet of you to say.'

Bryan's tone changed. 'No, not sweet. I meant it literally.'

'What are you talking about?'

'Really? You haven't heard, then?'

'What? I'm pleased with my website, so I'm not sure--'

'But you obviously haven't checked your email.'

Had she? Now that she thought about it, she'd just been painting to her heart's content. Not thinking overmuch. Reading a little. Perhaps not eating enough. And feeling a little lonely. But checking email? No. There had always been people to do that sort of thing.

'I suppose I haven't. Which is silly, of course, because you're quite right. Someone might want a painting or print or something, and I suppose I'm being really annoying by not answering.' She kept forgetting that she was beginning a new online business.

'Elena, I don't think you're going to be pleased, all right?' Bryan paused and she heard him sigh. 'It's been all over the newspapers. A story about you and that nasty piece of work, your ex-manager. Roman Giblin is claiming that the pair of you were having an affair and that's why you're...let's see, how did he phrase it? "No longer collaborating together to make beautiful art." For some reason, the tabloids are actually taking quite an interest, because he's also facing charges for some as-yet-unknown cybercrime. He wants to draw you into the line of fire alongside him. I'm guessing it's because we'll discover he withheld some funds from you along the way.'

'Oh, my goodness.' It was as though Roman and Nichola were right there in the room with her, and that desperate, helpless feeling came back.

'Because if you were having a relationship with him, then everyone may assume you would probably share all of the money made between you,' Bryan surmised. 'No one could accuse him of stealing, do you see?'

She did see. And she thought she may be sick.

WHENEVER THINGS DIDN'T GO ACCORDING to plan, Elena had always gotten the blame. She remembered a time when a prominent art critic had accused her of being immature in her approach to her work.

'What did you say to him?' Nichola had yelled at her in a hotel lift. 'How many times have I told you not to prattle on and on, showing people how stupid you are?'

She hadn't even been interviewed by the critic, but had apologised to Nichola.

'I'm sorry, Bryan. I'm having a hard time getting my head around this. What is it you're saying about my email?'

'Naturally, I expected people to contact you for your side of the story.'

Elena sighed. 'Oh, quite right. But they often make up a story, regardless.'

'I'm sure some of them do, yes. Not for his side of it, though. There was a video clip of Roman.'

So much for creating a new life here. Her past had caught her up. It was as if Nichola and Roman were here, shouting at her, and she felt drained of any strength to push back. Bryan was waiting for a response. 'What does the press seem to think of me? Are they labelling me a marriage-wrecker or something?'

'It may not be what everyone is reporting, but what I saw was something about, "Elena Dalca was ill for a time before she fled London," or something along those lines. And they've said they don't know where you are at present, but your website seems to indicate that you're "conducting your own career" and doesn't give information about your location. It seems as though public opinion about you could go either way.'

Thinking about the implications of what Bryan was saying, Elena walked out of the studio and stood on the lawn in front of the house, which was overgrown. The trees suddenly seemed full of watching eyes. She hurried to her cottage.

'Bryan, this is so strange. I feel like a fugitive from justice or something. Truly, I am the most boring person, and Roman is no more interesting than any bloke who can claim to be good at marketing. Why is the press even interested, do you think?'

'I can only give you my opinion, but here goes. It seems to me that your reputation has always been that of an innocent, talented girl who paints lovely things. Sunlight, children and nature. The fact that you're young and pretty...the press has made a story of less, I'm afraid.'

Then she remembered the message from her solicitor, Mr DeBoer. *Wanted to let you know I've filed legal action against Roman Giblin. An investments security officer rang to let me know of a fraudulent attempt by Giblin to access your funds.*

'I'm frightened.'

Bryan attempted to reassure her. 'Well, although he thinks he's coming off as a victim of bad circumstances, I'm afraid Roman Giblin is making things tougher on himself.'

'Do you think so? How?' She was grateful he couldn't see her. Her eyes had begun to water.

'As you said, Roman has done a good job marketing you all

along. It may be his undoing. We can't be sure how things will play out, but it seems to me that the press are less than convinced that you've jilted him, ruined his marriage, and led him off into a life of crime.' Bryan chuckled. 'Although they may not be so ready to let you off the hook if they knew about your mysterious alias, Tansy Button.'

'Ha ha.'

'You'll be all right, won't you?'

His jest about her alias made her realise she had made some progress since the first time she'd met Bryan. 'I don't know. I guess so. But I'm feeling fairly trepidatious about looking at my email.'

'Hmm. Yes, that could be very upsetting; it's hard to say what sort of nutters or aggressive journalists have tried to contact you.'

Elena considered calling Mr DeBoer and asking him for advice, but she felt she needed to get her head 'round all that had happened first.

'I've got an idea,' Bryan said enthusiastically. 'Dash sometimes hires people to take care of the websites he builds.'

'What do you mean?'

'Well, they upload new content, you know, like writing blog posts. And I'm fairly certain that some of them handle email as well. They answer emails using product manuals about the products being sold, or where the spare parts can be purchased and that sort of thing. I should think they could also shift these emails; maybe send some standard responses, whatever is appropriate. Anyway, I think there's probably someone Dash knows who would take a fee to go through the emails for you.'

'That would be brilliant.' She wondered if Dash would mind her contacting him, or if she ought to ask if Bryan minded.

Bryan added, 'But maybe you ought to see if my hunch is correct. Log on and see how many messages you have first.'

'Okay.'

Elena signed into the host website for her new email account.

'Bryan.'

'Yes?'

'I've got 1,436 emails.'

'Hells bells,' Bryan said, then whistled. 'I think you ought to ring Dash.'

Well, if Bryan thought she should... There was a tiny bit of silver in this dark cloud after all.

CHAPTER 21

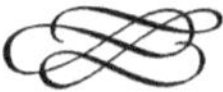

Elena had certainly wanted a reason to see Dash Minton again. But appealing for his help to manage a scandal wasn't the sort of thing she'd had in mind.

Bryan was correct; she ought to do something to respond to the onslaught of emails, even if they did have to do with Roman trying to draw her into a scandal.

She sent a message to Dash, asking to meet him at the coffee shop at his earliest convenience. She re-read it several times. She qualified her request, saying that Bryan had thought he may be able to help her with a sensitive "work-related issue." Satisfied, she sent off the message.

Elena put her phone aside. Now, what to do? Her cottage was in desperate need of a tidy, and she was in desperate need of some vigorous movement. She put on her favourite dance music by Clean Bandit--rousing pop that mimicked classical, called "Mozart's House" --which motivated her to scrub the bath...after watching a short video tutorial on how to clean a bath the correct way.

Two hours later, the cottage was spotless, and Dash hadn't

responded to her request. What if he didn't? Could she find help on her own? Perhaps she'd ask Bryan to get a referral from Dash, since he really wouldn't be providing the service anyway. Her spirits felt low and she decided to go to her studio. She'd been working on some sketches and had an idea about asking permission from Bess Seabury to have little Sarah pose for her.

She closed the cottage door behind her and then received a message: Dash wanted to meet her in an hour, if that would work for her? She replied and once again despaired that she had nothing but paint-stained work clothes to put on.

IDENTICAL TO THEIR FIRST MEETING, Dash was there before she arrived, sitting at the same table. She smiled at him and he simply tipped his chin. He had an empty mug and plate in front of him, bearing a few leftover crumbs.

There was no preamble. Dash gestured for her to sit down, and then said, 'Hello, Elena. How can I help you?'

His abruptness confused her. She felt she couldn't gather her thoughts and she mumbled, 'I'm having a problem.'

He waited, staring at her with beautiful eyes that she'd thought were simply green, but they had a bit of grey as well, trimmed with lush dark lashes. Her heart began to pound and her neck felt a bit hot and rashy. Elena had spent her life doing what was asked of her and never had much of a choice. Now she wasn't sure how to press on, given the low level of hostility that she sensed from Dash.

'I'm so sorry to have bothered you.' She stood and jogged unceremoniously towards the door, and out of the coffee shop. Safely in her vehicle, she struggled with the belt. It clicked in place and she started the engine. A movement caught her eye. It was Dash, coming out of the coffee house and approaching her door. He reached the vehicle and was standing close, glaring through the glass.

She opened the car window half-way. 'I am sorry, but I'm certain you'd rather not be bothered. My apologies for wasting your time.'

Rooted to the spot, Dash looked at his feet and then glanced the other way. She couldn't guess what he was thinking or why he seemed to be in two minds about the situation. She felt younger than her nineteen years; surely, Charlotte would be able to suss out what was going on here better than she.

Then he said, 'Please come back inside.'

Feeling utterly foolish, she followed him meekly back into the coffee shop. They sat down, and she took a few seconds to carefully hang her bag on the back of the chair.

He attempted to help her. 'Something to do with the website, I imagine?'

'Yes, exactly.'

'Can I get you a coffee?'

'Yes, please.'

He stood and went to the counter to order. The barista seemed to take an age. Dash returned and set down the mug. He had brought back the same drink he had ordered for her the last time. Taking a deep breath, she resolved to at least taste the coffee this time.

She immediately picked it up and drank. It was too hot and she dribbled some onto her lip, scorching both the inside and outside of her mouth. How clumsy.

'Oh,' he said, handing her a paper napkin. It was used but she didn't care, and she mopped up her mess, her mortification now complete. Spending the rest of her life in solitude was most assuredly the answer. Her last task of public life would be to ask this man, who obviously thought she was a clod, to help her with the trouble in which she found herself. She would get his help and get the website sorted. Then he would forget ever meeting her, and that would suit her perfectly.

It was time to explain why they were having this absurd

meeting. Her voice quivered a bit, but she concentrated on what needed to be said. No looking at the grey-green eyes again.

'My ex-manager is…well, he's been caught out doing something illegal. Consequently, there is a lawsuit in progress. Or, will be. Perhaps. Honestly, I'm not sure. A quick glance showed that journalists have contacted me. I mean, they've written to the website. I'm not sure what to do.'

Had that made any sense? Dash seemed to be waiting, in case she had something to add. Her lip pulsed and she wondered if a blister was forming.

'All right. Are you asking me to take down the contact page?'

'Um, no. Bryan said that you know people who deal with email. I don't want to read it all. I can't…it's all so negative, if you see what I mean.'

Apparently, humiliation became tolerable if you endured it at length. She felt less self-conscious, but the adrenalin or whatever it was kept her hands a bit shaky. A little joke even suddenly came to mind. 'I still haven't properly tasted the coffee!' She gave a little snort and looked at him.

He didn't reply or chuckle. He must think she was intoxicated or completely mad. No matter. This was her last time ever seeing him, then she could hide and paint and the whole world could just sod off. She wondered if some of the emails sent to her were, in fact, terribly hateful and if her silence would appear to prove her guilt. The thought of Roman being her lover was nauseating.

'Are you all right?'

She looked up at Dash. He seemed truly concerned. But she mustn't look at the green eyes.

'Yes, sorry,' she answered. 'A bit distracted.'

'I think I understand. Bryan probably indicated that I work with people who maintain website functions, answering email and so on. But I'm not sure this is within their usual scope.' He sat back in his chair and crossed his arms as though to distance himself from her problems. She could think of nothing to say; she only wished she hadn't come back in and carried on this conversation.

'It could be that they need a legal script to follow,' he added. 'They wouldn't want to make things worse.'

She hadn't thought of that.

It occurred to her that she hadn't thought of much. Her cottage was bare of food again, she hadn't any sensible clothes, her closest friends were solicitors and estate agents who had been paid to talk to her. And she'd just asked an incredibly lovely, handsome

man(also on the payroll, of course)to commit other people to coping with potentially injurious emails. It had only occurred to her this moment that she may be called into court, or worse, face some trumped-up charges. God only knew where this craziness with Roman was headed.

Dash cleared his throat and said, 'I don't mean to be insensitive.'

Really?

'It's simply, well, it's business, isn't it?' he continued. 'I don't think it's wise for me to carry on with finding people to answer your emails. At least until payment has been rendered.'

Elena stared at him, baffled.

'Your payment for the website design. The transaction failed.'

'What?'

Dash's voice took on a note of cynicism. 'I was a bit surprised as well. "Insufficient funds." Must be some sort of mistake?'

She felt poorly, like she had done when weaning off the medications. 'I suppose I need to check on some things. Please excuse me.' She stood and began walking to the door.

'Elena--' He snatched her arm.

'Let go.'

He did. And she walked out.

CHAPTER 22

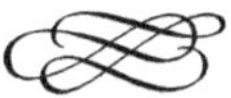

Dash was in a quandary. Things had gone from bad to worse with Elena yesterday, and he was at a loss as to how to fix it.

He was annoyed with her nearly as much as he was attracted to her.

Following some deliberation, he rang Bryan. They arranged to meet for coffee. As usual, Dash arrived early. He slid into his usual chair and drank his usual drink. His fingers had set to drumming on the table. Finally, Bryan's old car pulled into the car park.

Bryan stepped up to the counter and ordered a sandwich, got a coffee, and then sat down opposite Dash. Leaning back in his chair on two legs, he said, 'Mate. So, what happened?'

'Elena came to me for help, as you said she would.'

'And?'

'To be honest, she left in tears.'

Bryan's chair smacked to the floor. 'What did you say to her? She's a very vulnerable girl, you know.'

Dash raised his hands. 'I'm sorry. I am trying to make a

living, you know. You can't gloss over the fact that she owes me quite a bit of money.'

The coffee house employee brought Bryan's sandwich and he thanked her. He waited until she moved away. 'What did you say?'

Dash took a deep breath. 'It happened so quickly. She said she needed help with email. The next thing I knew, she was leaving. I followed her out to the car park and persuaded her to come back in. I was trying to inform her that her online payment hadn't worked. And then I tried to mend fences, but she was obviously distracted with something else.'

Bryan carried on chewing his sandwich. Dash was getting the vibe that Bryan thought it was his fault. Dash said, 'The whole exchange was a bit too dramatic for my liking. Does she carry on like that often?'

'Dash...' Bryan put his sandwich down.

Dash sighed. 'Look, all I meant to say is that she needed legal advice. These emails weren't going to be the usual, so I suggested her solicitor needed to okay the team's response.'

'That's a good idea. And you want me to believe that you made this excellent suggestion and then she was unreasonable. Why?'

Dash wanted to say, "Hell if I know why," but he suspected that he did know why. And Bryan wasn't going to let it go. 'I bought her a coffee, and then she explained that her manager or some bloke was brought up on charges or something.'

Bryan's eyebrow went up as if to say, 'And?'

'Look, she probably didn't like the fact that, basically, I refused to help. But do the people I work with deserve to get caught up in some legal problem? Not to mention,' Dash said, warming to the subject, 'I'm not going to come to the rescue of someone who acts totally unhinged instead of just taking out her phone and making a payment.'

'Oh, so that's the decisive point at issue. Money.' Bryan took a bite of his lunch.

'I was trying to inform her that her online payment hadn't worked. And, yes, there were tears and running out the door. You'll fix it?'

Bryan looked at him. 'Why should I? You're able to speak to your own clients.'

Dash leaned back and crossed his arms. 'You got me into this. You told her to phone me with a problem I can't solve.'

'Can't or won't?' Bryan shot back.

'You don't know the half of it,' Dash exclaimed. 'She wrote a bad cheque for the piece I put up for auction.'

'She bid on your work?'

'Not very endearing when you don't pay for it.'

'Fine. I'll ring her and tell her that you didn't mean to upset her,' Bryan said. 'Since that's all there is to it, and, according to you, she's unhinged.'

Dash ignored the comment and grasped at his escape. 'Thanks. Hopefully, that will help me get paid.'

'Right.'

Dash pulled out his phone and thumbed around a bit. 'I may as well give you the name of the guy who provides the website and email support services. No need for me to stick my nose in again. Elena and her solicitor can contact them directly.'

Bryan put his sandwich down. 'If that's all that needs doing, you can send that along to her. But you don't seem to want to have any contact with her. Why would that be? Just because she was a bit overwrought?'

Dash began fidgeting again, shaking his leg beneath the table. 'Perhaps we pretend that you don't need to know every detail. Because it's irrelevant.'

'My, we are a bit prickly. I may think *you're* unhinged.'

'Seriously, Bryan, you know I hate it when you try to psychoanalyse.'

'But it's such good fun.' Bryan leaned forward slightly and gave Dash's upper arm a gentle punch. 'I'm just a bit confused, that's all. I thought, with both of you being artists, that you'd hit it off.'

'Hardly.'

'How so?' Bryan asked.

'We're very different.'

'Are you telling me that because you work with metal and wood, all the macho materials, and she paints, that you've nothing in common? Don't look at me like that. No cheek intended, I really don't understand.'

'We have nothing in common because of money.'

'You mean, she has quite a lot of it, and you don't. Not in her league, perhaps, but you're doing really well for yourself, Dash.'

'No. And, apparently, it doesn't matter if she has it, because she's too above it all to pay her bills. But that's not the point. It's because she's a *commercial* artist. And I'm not for sale.'

Bryan sat for a moment, processing. 'Mmm, no. Sorry, I don't get it. You know I'm a bit thick, so humour me. You're a marketing genius and your stuff is for sale on the internet, but you're not commercial?'

'I have to live.'

'You could live on your website and marketing designs, and save the other stuff for museums. Honestly, mate, I'm just trying to get my head 'round it.'

Dash pulled his fingers through his hair. At this rate, he'd be better off making some enemies. Surely, they'd be easier to get on with than the people he counted as friends. 'I see why you don't grasp it, Bryan. Yet, the difference is so bloody obvious.'

'Face it, Dash. You conduct art trade. Same difference.'

Dash paused. 'No, Bryan. I don't consider myself commercial. Yes, my art is for sale and I hope people buy it and enjoy it. When I sell a piece, I think of it as "rehoming" my art, sort of like an adoption process. Sure, I've got a measurable cost that's represented in materials, sweat equity, my time. But people like Elena, and her management group'--he began counting off on his fingers--'and her solicitor and her press agents and her gallery-owners-in-everybody's-pockets, all of the people it takes to be "Elena Dalca" live in an entirely different universe to me.' Dash leaned forward, his wrists crossed on the table and looked intently at Bryan, willing him to understand the vital point. 'I'm not saying that Elena doesn't have talent. I think her work is good. But she's part of "the system." She does what's commercially viable.'

'Okay. I think I get what you're trying to say. However, I'm not sure making millions is truly beneath you.'

Dash sighed and gazed out the window. Could this conversation become any more tedious? Why wouldn't Bryan leave it? Maybe he was interested in Elena romantically. Although he couldn't see Bryan breaking up with Theresa; they'd been together since they were fifteen.

'It could've been you instead of Elena. You know you're a handsome bloke, Dash. You'd be right at home on the telly, wouldn't you? You have an interesting life story, and a unique sort of art to sell. If a management group approached you and wanted to take you "global" or whatever it is they say, you're telling me you wouldn't even think about it?'

'I'd be lying if I said I wouldn't think about it. I mean, what's Elena Dalca worth—like seventeen million pounds or something? Which makes it all the more interesting that I'm waiting for my paycheque. I digress. It's tempting to think about grabbing that kind of cash if someone offers up a contract, but I hope I wouldn't sign.'

'And not signing gives you some sort of purity in your work or something?'

'Just so.' Finally, he'd gotten through. 'It's an artists' integrity to focus on the work. To "express" your art, not "produce" it on schedule and according to trend.'

'You think Elena is a hack.'

Dash crossed his arms. 'It's not personal. We just don't have much in common.'

'I was the first person she met when she came here last month,' Bryan said. 'And I can't agree with you. She struck me as one of the most genuine people I'd ever met.'

Maybe Bryan did want to date her. 'Genuine? She lied. She gave you a false name, with some cock and bull story about a family member that doesn't exist.'

Bryan smiled. There was no arguing with the facts. 'Well, she obviously has a high opinion of you, Dash. Bidding on your work at the auction so that she could take home one of your sculptures. I've a feeling it was the highest bid of the evening, wasn't it?'

'But that's telling, isn't it? Like you said, Bryan, she just got here last month. She doesn't care about the hospital fund. I contributed art for the cause; she showed up and threw money around. Thankfully, the bidders' names weren't made public, or she probably would've set us all down in a mess-with-the-press.'

'Do you know what, Dash?' Bryan said with a laugh. 'I think you may just be jealous of her success.'

Dash shook his head. Best to leave the conversation where it stood. He wouldn't tell Bryan his very personal reason for attempting to avoid Elena Dalca.

It wasn't about his not getting paid.

It wasn't about her commercial success or his lack of it.

It was about protecting his heart now that he was finally free of the pain.

CHAPTER 23

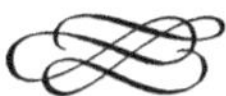

Elena had been on the phone for an interminable length of time. The answers given to her questions were dire.

'I'm sorry, Miss Dalca. The balance in the account is negative ninety-seven pounds. There was a service charge exacted, you see, and that is why the balance is below zero. Would you like to pay the ninety-seven-pound charge? I could receive your credit card payment now.'

'But...I don't understand.'

The customer service person, a young man by the name of Mr Castille, was unable to provide further assistance at this time. He was in the process of giving her a number to reach another department, but Elena terminated the conversation.

She had hung up on Mr Castille. She'd been so rude. She sat quite still on her sofa, speechless.

It was some minutes later that she heard a knock on the door of her cottage. Elena didn't move. She simply couldn't. Her energy was completely engaged in getting her head around her new reality.

'Elena!' the person called and knocked on her door with a fresh show of force.

She roused herself and shuffled to the door to find Veronica Hayward standing on her doorstep. The vicar's wife wore a concerned expression, and she didn't wait for Elena to invite her in.

'Oh, you poor lamb! I can see by your face that my suspicions are correct. He's taken everything, hasn't he?'

Elena crumpled at hearing the truth spoken by a person who cared for her. The compassion struck her deeply, and she leaned into Veronica's embrace and sobbed.

As Elena's weeping diminished to swollen eyes and humiliation, the vicar's wife guided her over to the sofa. Wiping her nose on her sleeve, Elena uttered, 'I don't even have any tea to offer you.' This confession brought a few fresh sobs, whilst Veronica patted Elena on the arm. Then Elena said, 'How did you know?'

Veronica was silent for a few moments. 'No one else knows this, and you mustn't mention it, all right?'

Elena sniffed and nodded.

'A lifetime ago, I was in the SIS.'

Elena had no idea what she meant. 'What?'

Veronica explained, 'The Secret Intelligence Service. Essentially, I worked for our government in different parts of the world, as a targeter, part of a counter-terrorism team. I was able to assess a breach in security by following money trails.'

'Oh.'

Veronica smiled gently at Elena and reached out to brush her hair from where a strand had stuck to her moist cheek. 'Domestic security is rather easy to work out. The person stealing has learnt inside information about the person he's stealing from.'

Elena sprouted fresh tears.

Veronica continued, 'I was reasonably sure, as I've observed

Roman Giblin's behaviour and heard tiny clues in the press, that he's been caught out trying to steal from you.'

'Yes. He has.'

'But what I understand, that perhaps no one else does yet, is that he didn't have to steal from you. Did he?'

Elena's head began to pound. 'I don't really know. I mean, I just can't understand. I wasn't even sure who to call.'

'Elena, did you sign any legal papers in the last year?'

'No. That is, nothing but the usual tax forms from the accountant.'

'Hmm.' Veronica stood up from the sofa. She walked over towards the fireplace and rested her hand on the mantel. Elena noticed, then, just how cold the room was. She had burnt through the small stack of fake logs from the supermarket. The tiny Aga wasn't taking the chill off today.

'What would I have been signing?' Elena's voice reflected how feeble she felt, even though she couldn't yet understand just what was happening.

Veronica took a deep breath and went back to her place on the sofa. 'As a minor, it's almost certain that your guardian had collected your earnings in a trust. That is, an account that he shared with you.'

'And when I became of age?'

'Yes, you understand. You should've claimed the trust for your sole use.'

Elena still wasn't sure she understood. 'But I recently transferred money from the trust. Thousands and thousands of pounds. It wasn't any problem.'

'My guess is that you withdrew money and moved it to a new place, a fresh account.'

'Yes, that's right. Enough money to pay for this property. And to buy my car. To live on for a little while.'

'And now it's gone,' Veronica said softly. 'The money in your new account.'

'Yes, because I thought I could transfer more from the fund as I needed it.

Veronica frowned. 'But he's cleaned out the balance from the original fund, hasn't he?'

Light dawned. Elena said, 'Yes. But my solicitor brought him up on charges. He's in trouble.'

'I'm so sorry, darling,' Veronica said. 'It was wrong of Roman to try to access your new account, the one you've been using to pay for your new life, and it was correct that charges be brought against him. But your original trust fund--with the lion's share of cash--was his as well as yours. You see, the worst part of this is he's stolen nothing, technically speaking. And he'll have known you couldn't afford to bring him to court to argue the point.'

Panic coursed through Elena's body, pricking her fingertips with cold pain and seizing her throat.

She had seventy-nine pounds in her handbag. How would she pay her bills? Or keep herself in art supplies? The land taxes would be very high on the new property, not to mention the money withdrawn from the trust fund. She had no money to give to Dash for her website. No money to buy food beyond the next week.

Veronica reached out and put a hand on Elena's shoulder. 'You are going to get through this. Don't fear. Don't give up your courage and let Roman Giblin win.'

Elena had no words, only tears.

CHAPTER 24

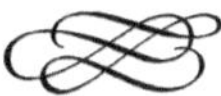

Willa felt a bit odd about inviting Elena for a meal. She had thought of it several weeks ago when they'd met for the first time at Rhys' food stall in the library. But she'd left it too long, and now it would seem as though cooking for her was to win her over, given what she wanted to discuss.

Willa had become quite keen on the idea of reinstating the bed and breakfast in Elena's house.

Oliver was supportive. 'I can see that this would be a good fit for you, sweetie,' he said. 'You love to cook. It would also be a creative endeavour, decorating the house and so forth.'

'But would it be good for us, Oliver? That's what I need to know.'

'Well, I certainly don't see any harm in it, so long as you're not making yourself miserable with impossible deadlines to get it all done. I hope to finally be able to spend some time with you.'

'Doing what?'

Oliver laughed.

'No, Oliver, in all seriousness, I've missed you too. But, I mean, once we return from our honeymoon and life starts to take on a more normal pace, then what?'

'Willa--'

'Oliver, I'm not trying to dredge up an old quarrel. What I mean to ask is, would you consider working with me on this bed and breakfast project? Could that be an enjoyable adventure for both of us? Do you have any interest at all? Before you say anything, I'm not asking to pressure you, or cause this to be some sort of ultimatum for my pursuing it. I'm asking because I really don't know if you think it would be fun.'

'I do, actually.'

'Really? Oh, Oliver, that's wonderful. Are you sure?'

He paused. 'Yes, I think so. When my mum was stumped over things to do with the Hall or letting the cottages, she always asked my opinion. Father and Penelope wouldn't help her, so she came to me. I think she might say we've made a pretty good team at that sort of thing. We've refurbished several properties, actually.'

'I didn't know that about you.'

'I'm glad to pleasantly surprise you,' he replied. 'Besides, I think I'll be funding this venture, so I'll want to be on hand to sign the cheques.'

'I love you.'

'I love you too, Willa. *Our* bed and breakfast will be brilliant.'

'Well, maybe. I haven't broken it to the owner yet. She may very well tell me to bugger off.'

'If she does, then we can look for another place. Or you'll find a project to take on that you want even more. It's all good, isn't it?'

Having Oliver's support had made her glad that she had the wedding plans sorted. Actually, Mollie had been the voice of reason there.

'Just get married at the church, Willa. Like a normal girl,' she'd said. Willa had had no choice, really, but to dry her eyes and stop dramatising. She'd smiled weakly at her sister and had to admit that moving the wedding from Myndcroft Hall--and all of the lofty expectations created in such an esteemed venue--made things quite a lot simpler. More her style, really.

So, now she could begin to make a list of what she would discuss with Elena.

But first, Willa wanted to work out Roni's new menus as soon as possible. She dreaded telling Roni that she wanted to be her consultant. Hopefully, the new menus would help assure Roni that the new role was a good idea. She planned to tell Roni that she would email her details about each menu item and pricing, and they could schedule a taste test. And by the time Willa had got all that worked out, she would probably need to shelve everything in order to enjoy her wedding and honeymoon, or Oliver wasn't going to be at all happy with her.

It was all so exciting.

Dinner this evening would be a recipe test of chicken and leek pie for Roni's early autumn menu, alongside a caramel and croissant bread pudding. She also had a salad in mind which she hadn't quite worked out yet. She knew she wanted to use dried cranberries sprinkled on it, but had forgotten to put the cranberries on her shopping list. She made a note to buy them, and then she had a sudden inspiration for using shaved Brussels sprouts in some way, and made a note of that too.

She'd just put together the bread pudding when she heard a car door shut.

Elena.

Willa felt a few butterflies. Perhaps this evening wasn't appropriate for mentioning Willa's B&B idea. They'd only met Elena once or twice; the poor girl may feel that they were somehow ganging up on her. Elena hadn't even met Oliver. Perhaps she ought to give the whole subject a miss until later.

. . .

Elena drove the short distance up the hill and turned left into the farmyard. She pulled to the side where there was a small gravel car park and turned off her vehicle. She sat for a moment, gathering her strength. Since yesterday, after Veronica had revealed the reality of Elena's financial circumstances, everything had seemed like a monumental effort. She hadn't even been able to go to her studio this morning. She knew she must eat, and that was one of the reasons she'd accepted Willa's dinner invitation. Her empty stomach grumbled as though to reinforce the point in her thoughts.

Elena glanced around Hilltop Farm. There were several barns, one old stone, one that looked like a new construction. The farmhouse appeared to not be very old, and it was large. There was a dog watching her with interest from the porch. If he wanted to come and devour her, he was welcome. She hardly cared.

The people inside the house, on the other hand, were much more intimidating. She took a deep breath and climbed out of her vehicle into the rain.

Willa opened the door. 'Elena! Please come in.'Do you want me to take your jacket? I'll hang it on the range handle and it'll dry in a mo.'

Elena was taken aback by the question for a second, and then said, 'Oh, yes.' She wriggled out of the wet garment. Alarmingly, Elena felt like crying; Willa was kind, and the house was warm and welcoming. The comfort and caring melted her inside. Luckily, her hair covered the side of her face, and Willa was bustling around, relieving her of her coat, and didn't notice Elena's emotions welling up. It was the first time a friend had asked her to a home cooked meal in a very long time.

'Come on through.'

Elena wiped away a stray tear. 'It smells heavenly. I appreciate you asking me.'

'Actually, you're helping me,' Willa chirped. 'The more feedback I have for developing recipes. the better. Usually, it's a good thing to have a family who will eat anything, but not so good when you want to perfect something for a restaurant.'

'Well, if it tastes as good as it smells, we're in for a treat.'

Willa hung Elena's jacket on the rail of the Aga and turned to smile her thanks. 'You probably can guess that farming schedules don't run exactly by the clock. Rhys and Mollie should be in shortly, though. Shall we go ahead and sit down while we wait for them?'

The kitchen's open-plan dining area was part of the sitting room beyond. Elena looked around. It was a large, inviting space. There was a big sofa with lots of cushions, and four comfy chairs. A wide, low table was spread with magazines. In the corner stood a towering dresser, and there were cheerful houseplants here and there. Now that Elena had gotten past the tears, she simply felt relaxed and happy. She followed Willa in sitting on the sofa.

Willa gestured to Elena's jacket hanging on the range and said, 'I can imagine you don't have much in the way of the kind of clothes needed up here.'

'I seemed to pop in and out of cars in London, so I didn't have to bother about the weather,' Elena admitted. 'And I had to wear lots of swishy sorts of things for functions, all of which I left behind. So I find myself completely caught out.'

'Absolutely. For warm things, like a jacket, quilted gilet, or maybe fleece, try Countrywide,' Willa said. 'And for everything else, Tuesday's. Both are in Ludlow. It's a little bit of a drive, but they've got anything you'd want and the prices are excellent.'

It seemed to Elena that Willa felt silly saying that last bit and she smiled. If Willa only knew… Even discount prices weren't manageable at the moment.

'Maybe I'm mistaken,' Willa said, 'but you don't seem to me

the type to want to spend five hundred pounds on a plain white blouse and wanting everyone in the village to know how dear it was.'

'You're right!' Elena confirmed. They laughed.

'Thanks,' Elena said. 'I've been wanting to see Ludlow, anyway.'

'I don't know if you prefer shopping on your own, but if not, I'll be going up next week. Probably on Thursday, around three? Just to see my mum. Of course, her husband, Sam, and their adorable baby will be there, and possibly my younger sister. You're welcome to come along with me. I could shop with you, or drop you off and do some errands or something. Then we could visit my mum, eat with them at five, and then come home.'

'I've never really shopped on my own before. I know it sounds silly, and it's rather embarrassing, actually.' Elena didn't want to pass up the invitation, even if she wouldn't have the money to shop. She would wait to mention that to Willa. 'I could probably use some shopping advice. But just going to see your family would be lovely.'

'Helping Phoebe--that's our fashionista, fifteen-year-old sister--has practically rendered me a professional.'

They heard the boot room door open. Mollie appeared in the kitchen, with Rhys following close behind.

'Sorry we're running late, Willa,' Mollie said. 'Hi, Elena. We're never late to dinner unless company comes, you know. My apologies.'

'Not at all,' Elena said, with a hello to Rhys. The group moved towards the kitchen table as Willa removed a large dish from the oven. She was about to set the dish down on a heat guard just as Mollie grinned and said, 'Well, what did you say, Elena? Are you going to let my sister take over your whacking great house?'

Elena realised her mouth had gone slack and pressed it closed. Willa's face suggested the desire to dump the pie into her sister's lap.

Placing the steaming pie onto the table, Willa said, 'Mollie. I actually hadn't mentioned my idea to Elena yet.'

Mollie's brows went up in an "uh-oh" expression.

Rhys tried to salvage the situation. 'Elena, we're glad that you came over this evening to give us all a chance to chat. Whether you want to go along with Willa's ideas for your property or not--and, actually, she usually has good ideas--we were glad to finally meet you at the farmer's market. It's such a small community here in Marris Mynd, yet it can feel a bit awkward, stepping into village life.'

'Yes, I'm glad too.' Elena smiled graciously, not feeling at all cross, merely puzzled. Willa immediately grinned with relief, but Elena guessed that she was none too pleased with Mollie. She had seen Willa, peripherally, shoot a look at her sister while Rhys was talking. Mollie's expression, in return, was as good as saying, 'Well, you sat here talking for ages. It wasn't my fault.'

A hush fell around the table as Willa began to serve the pie.

Elena made an effort. 'I'd heard about your family from Charlotte Seabury.'

'Oh, we love Charlotte,' Mollie said. 'She's helped out here with the goats.'

Her serving duties done, Willa took a seat. She turned to Elena and said, 'My apologies for the awkwardness.'

'No problem, Willa. This pie is delicious. I wouldn't change a thing.'

'Nor would I,' said Rhys, taking a big mouthful.

'Mollie?'

'It's perfect.' Mollie looked at her sister, whom she knew was still irritated. 'And don't get testy because we don't have a suggestion.'

Willa tasted it herself and had to agree. 'It's a simple recipe, but with the sophisticated filo pastry on the top it's just the sort of pie to sell well at the tea shop.'

'Now you have to figure out how to increase it,' Mollie said.

Willa turned to Elena and explained. 'It defies reason, but just tripling and quadrupling ingredient amounts doesn't always work, and the flavour profile can go horribly wrong.'

Elena nodded, 'I can't imagine developing a recipe. And I'm eager to hear your idea, Willa.'

'You're not offended that I have one?'

'Not at all. I bought the property sight unseen. For me, the value of it is in the studio. My first priority was a place to work, and that was the only property for miles that had a studio, especially one with adequate space and lighting.'

'I feel better hearing that,' Willa said, smiling. 'And since you're not annoyed, I must confess that the idea originally came from Veronica Hayward.'

'Oh, the vicar's wife?' Elena looked thoughtful. Somehow, that doesn't surprise me.' They shared a laugh.

Willa told Elena about Veronica's idea of reinstating the bed and breakfast in the main house. 'Apparently, the Smiths had built up a clientele over time of people who wanted views, quiet, and good food. However, my future father-in-law is developing a golf course in Pulverbridge, and now we have Rhys holding a farmer's market. These are the sort of changes that draw people in.'

'Yes, I can imagine.'

Willa seemed energised by talking about the project. 'Also, Veronica shared with me that some other people may benefit from having the B&B running again.'

Elena immediately looked up. 'Bess Seabury.'

'How did you know?'

'She came over with her girls. She said she had been the housekeeper.'

'I guess the closing impacted their family finances quite a lot,' Willa said.

Little did Willa know, but Elena could relate to a loss of finances. She found herself constantly thinking about money, and even this evening, in the company of these lovely people, the topic somehow still remained on the fringe of her thoughts.

'But perhaps you really need your privacy, Elena. I've had enough people poke their nose into my kitchen at the tearoom to know that guests can be nosy and tend to wander into areas they're not supposed to go. And you can't cover the windows of your studio to keep them out.'

'That's a sticking point, I have to admit. But on the other hand, it's been a bit…lonely.' Willa laid her hand across Elena's arm. The simple gesture didn't threaten tears this time, but instead made Elena feel valued, part of a community, with her neighbours seated around the table.

'We're really glad we have each other, Elena,' Mollie said. 'I'd hate farming here by myself, and I'm a fairly independent person.'

Rhys put his arm around his wife and gave her shoulders a squeeze, indicating that he was glad not to be on his own as well.

'When do I need to make a decision?' Elena asked.

'Oh, my goodness! Well, not anytime soon, as I don't want to pressure you,' Willa said. 'You know I'm getting married in June. Then we're going away on a long honeymoon. And the more I think about it, the more I imagine that Oliver won't want to live there, so we'll probably be a mile down the road at his parents' place.'

'It's not like it sounds,' Mollie said sarcastically. 'They've got like twenty rooms or something. The missus here will have her own wing.'

Elena raised her brows and Willa giggled. 'Anyway, maybe we can talk more about it at the end of the summer?'

'Okay, sure,' Elena said.

'Brilliant. Let's taste the pudding and see if it's any good.'

CHAPTER 25

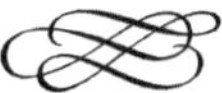

'I'm afraid that it's one of those days when Rhys needs his pickup for deliveries,' Willa apologised. 'Fingers crossed, the old Land Rover will get us to Ludlow without being temperamental.'

'We can take my car if you'd rather.' Elena dug in her pocket and produced the keys. 'Why don't you drive, since you know where we're going?'

'Your MPV looks brand new. Are you sure?'

'Positive.'

Willa took the wheel. She thought that Elena looked exhausted; perhaps that was another reason she didn't want to drive. Willa did up the belt.

'At least we're the same height, so no having to move the seat around. Mollie and Rhys are so much taller than me that I'm constantly readjusting.'

They chatted easily on the way to Ludlow.

'How long ago did your father pass away?'

Willa did the maths. 'About thirteen years ago, now. My mum and Sam got married almost three years ago. Phoebe was very small when our dad had his accident, and she doesn't remember him at all. I remember him only a little, but Mollie's memories are quite clear. She and dad were very close.'

'Did that make you feel left out?'

'It has, a little.'

Willa found Elena very easy to talk to. In a way, she was uncomplicated, like someone younger than their age. But Willa suspected that, in reality, Elena's life had been as much a tangle as anyone's.

She asked Elena, 'And your parents?'

'I don't know. I never knew them.'

'Were you an orphan?'

'For some reason, that's such a Dickensian word, isn't it? True, though. Me and Oliver Twist.' The girls shared a laugh. Then Elena added, 'I was given over to a woman who brought me to England.'

'So, you were adopted?' Willa couldn't imagine not knowing her mother and father or sisters—or almost everyone in the village and nearby, for that matter.

'Not really. Honestly, I don't know if the woman who brought me here was considered a sort of legal guardian or just a temporary person to transport me. But she was horrible. She was an old woman called Réka Lupei. Her name means "wolf" and she was that intimidating; I remember thinking she was actually a wolf dressed as a granny in the daytime, you know, like in Red Riding Hood.'

'She sounds ghastly.'

'She was. Fortunately, after we arrived in England, I was quickly sent off to a boarding school. I made friends and went home with them at the holidays, and I didn't really know to whom I belonged. Then, at the age of nine, my manager and his wife sort of materialised and became my guardians.'

'And you didn't see the wolf-lady again?'

'No. I think they gave her money and she disappeared. I've asked, but they refused to tell me anything, advising me not to be so morbid and curious about my sad life, and emphasising how I would still be in an orphanage without their patronage.'

'Don't take this the wrong way,' Willa said, 'but it sounds like something from a film.'

'Doesn't it? I agree, even though it actually happened to me. Anyway, my manager could see that I had an unusual talent for my age, so he began showing my work. Then on to exhibiting at galleries, television shows, and that sort of thing.'

'Will you continue doing all of that?' Willa hadn't been sure how to ask the question more intelligently. "Will you continue being a famous person?" really sounded awful. But clearly, now that Elena was of age and means, she had a choice.

'No. I want to continue as an artist, but not in a way that feels like I'm a circus performer. We travelled the world, marketing my work—and me, really—to one country at a time. And then we'd begin the cycle again. It was exhausting, but I also experienced a lot of great things. It's more about the art for me, though.'

Willa thought about this. The closest example she had given any thought to was how the Duchess of Cambridge must feel, having to "be Kate Middleton," a sort of travelling global commodity. She imagined it would be wrought with challenges.

'I hope I didn't pry,' Willa said.

'Oh, no, not at all. It's refreshing to talk with people who haven't read about me and think they know me. And to be with people who don't want anything from me.'

'I wish I could honestly fit in that category! I've just told you I want your house.'

Elena started giggling. 'You know what I mean, though. And I don't really care about that house. It's just coming to terms with the guests. That would be the part I'm not sure of.'

'I know,' Willa agreed. 'That's what concerns me, too.'

. . .

Elena found Willa's family in Ludlow just as warm and lovely as Willa's sister and brother-in-law. They sat around the dinner table, the meal finished but everyone enjoying one another's company.

'We've finished another book, Willa,' said Sam, a writer of textbooks. Sam was the nicest sort of man, gentle and so happy with his new little family. Lisa's easy-going personality complemented him.

'It's an amazing achievement, as sleep deprived as we've been,' Lisa said. Their two-and-a-half-year-old son, Elliot, sat on Lisa's lap, growing sleepy.

Willa's younger sister, Phoebe, had missed the family meal because she'd been out earlier with friends. Now, Phoebe sat nearby, deeply engrossed in her phone, her long silky blonde hair curtaining her face. Elena wondered if she ought to say something to Phoebe about being Charlotte's neighbour. It was difficult to imagine Charlotte, so open-natured and slightly awkward, being close friends with the doll-like Phoebe, who favoured her mother in features and figure. Elena recalled that Charlotte had said Phoebe was very popular at her school. When Phoebe arrived home and spoke to Elena, she was much like her sister, Willa, personable and intelligent.

'Congratulations on your book,' Willa said to Sam and her mother. 'Mum, you would've loved seeing the library full of people again.Our second farmer's market really pulled in a lot of visitors.'

'I'm looking forward to coming this weekend,' Lisa said.

'That's how we met Elena,' Willa said, drawing Elena into the conversation. Elena had been quiet, and it seemed at times Willa had forgotten she was there, which was fine with Elena. She supposed a little of that was normal when joining a family dinner. The truth was, Elena didn't know. She'd spent little time in family settings.

'Rhys' produce was lovely,' Elena said, making another effort.

'I met the "newlyweds."' They laughed, as everyone was well-familiar with the recently betrothed couple.

'Willa, didn't you say something about them having a table?' Sam asked.

'Mrs Ballard is selling her knitting.'

'I bought a throw for my sofa, and she gifted me a hat,' Elena added. 'It was so kind of her, and I've actually used both quite a bit.'

'Wonderful!' Lisa said. 'I hope everyone wants to participate and you'll have more tables as time goes on.'

'Rhys has had a number of people enquire about space already,' Willa explained. 'One gentleman wants to sell beer, but Rhys needs to check on the details about that. Bess is bringing her jams and chutneys beginning this weekend. Another lady wants to come from Shrewsbury and bring furniture and home items. And Dash is interested in bringing some artwork.'

'He's a brilliant artist.' Lisa turned to Elena, 'Do you happen to have met Dash? You're an artist, too, I understand.'

'Yes, and yes,' Elena said. She blushed and was at a loss for words.

Willa didn't seem to notice. She asked, 'Really? How do you know Dash?'

Elena replied, 'He did my website,' but offered nothing else.

'He's our designer, too,' Willa said. 'He's done the labels for Mollie's cheeses, and they won an award at some large food show in Birmingham.'

'That poor boy has been through so much,' Lisa said.

'Who's this?' Sam asked.

'Dashiell--oh, I've forgotten his surname, Willa.'

'Minton.'

'Yes, that's right. He was engaged to be married, but she was killed whilst visiting in some other country. I'm glad to hear he's joining the farmer's market. Whenever he can get out and meet people it ought to help.'

'But Mum, that's been two years ago now.'

'Has it really?' Lisa said. She laughed, 'I suppose when you have a baby, you lose touch with the wider community.'

Willa glanced at Elena. Instead of joining in the laughter, she looked positively stricken. Perhaps she was feeling poorly.

'Mum, it's been so wonderful to see you all, but we've stayed a bit longer than I told Elena we'd be. I think we ought to be going.'

Elena didn't contradict the suggestion, but politely thanked Sam and Lisa for the meal, and reiterated how nice it was to meet them.

WHEN THEY HAD BEEN in the car chatting for some minutes, Willa asked Elena, 'You didn't know about Dash's fiancée?'

'No,' she said. 'What was she like?'

'She was a primary school teacher, very sweet. Bess Seabury is her aunt, but I didn't know her well.'

Elena was quiet for a moment. Then she asked, 'What did she look like?'

'Sort of like me, really. Long blonde hair. She was petite, like us.' Willa smiled at her in the darkening car. 'Why would you ask that?'

'Because I think I said something wrong about a piece of art that Dash made to look like her. I'm certain it hit a nerve.'

Willa said, 'Oh, surely not? What could you have said that would've been so awful?'

'Honestly, I don't remember exactly. I was distracted, because I sensed something very different about that piece. It was an ethereal fairy, but so real, as though one moment she'd been a normal person and the next moment was frozen by magic or something. I'm sorry, I know I sound as though I'm being fanciful. But, Willa, if you could've seen his face. I'm not sure he'll ever forgive me.'

CHAPTER 26

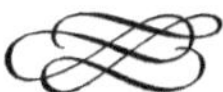

Elena was knackered the following day. She'd enjoyed Willa's company and sharing another family dinner with her; however, the conversation about Dash had caught her unawares, and the stress of figuring out what to do about her finances had kept her from a good night's rest. She was still mulling over Veronica's suggestions about reinstating Bytheway as a bed and breakfast. Willa seemed to want to shelf the conversation until after her wedding, so Elena needed to earn income another way until then.

Nevertheless, the calendar turned to April and the morning was clear and bathed in sunshine. The cherry trees that lined up the path to her studio had been forming tight pink buds, and the warmth brought the first blossoms. Elena lingered by the flowering trees, studying the candyfloss-coloured blooms. Surely, cherries were the loveliest of trees. Just looking at them re-energised her. She snapped a few photos. Perhaps when she painted Sarah Seabury, she would use the cherry trees as a backdrop. The idea inspired her, and suddenly a composition formed in her head: Sarah walking through the little avenue of trees in full bloom. She would ring Bess and schedule a time for

Sarah to come over. Her age would keep Sarah from wanting to pose for very long, but Elena could do some quick sketches and take photographs for reference. Often, though, when she saw the subject matter in real life, the image would impress upon her mind until she finished painting.

She was absorbed in taking photos of the ornamental trees when a vehicle pulled up in the drive. It was a white SUV, and a man with dark hair sat behind the wheel. Elena froze. She wanted to run to her studio but felt rooted to the ground.

The vehicle door opened, then was slammed shut, causing her to shudder. The man walked around the front of the vehicle, and she gasped in relief. It was Dash.

He approached her. 'Elena. Are you all right?'

'I didn't know who you were.' She wiped her eyes. She felt foolish, but sometimes a fright brought tears to her eyes.

'My apologies. I should've thought to ring you first.' Dash lifted and dropped his hands in a gesture of helplessness and looked uncomfortable.

She must get control of her emotions and do something to put him at ease. 'Won't you come in for a cup of tea? My cottage is on the other side of the drive.'

He gave her a shallow nod.

She paced towards the cottage, giving a wide berth as she passed him to lead the way. The cottage was spotlessly tidy from the weekend deep clean, and she was glad she'd put away things in the loo and made her bed today. Opening the door, she realised that her home had never looked better. The sunshine pouring in the windows made it even more inviting than usual.

Dash followed her in and was looking around as Elena went immediately to the kettle and filled it for tea. Then, she remembered that she hadn't any. Neither had she any coffee, or biscuits. He'd walked to the window by the fireplace and stood there looking out. It was similar to the stance that Veronica had taken by the fireplace, and it gave Elena the impression that different people, like characters, were acting out scenes with her in the cottage. She wondered what to say to him.

Surely, he was here to talk about money. But she imagined that Dash wouldn't know just how desperate her finances had become. Veronica was as safe as houses; she wouldn't have spread the story of Elena's financial ruin around the village. After all, Veronica was literally a professional regarding these matters.

But then Elena remembered that her general financial ruin wasn't the point at all. She owed Dash money for building her website. She felt nervous, with little darts shooting through her tummy. What should she do? The "store" part of the website wasn't yet finished, so she was unable to sell anything yet, which would have helped her to pay him. Of course, he must realise that already.

The water came to the boil. 'I'm not very civilised and don't sit at the dining table much.'

Well, Elena thought to herself, *that was a ridiculous observation to share.*

Turning from the window, his hands in his pockets, Dash carefully surveyed the cottage.

Perhaps there's something here I ought to sell to pay for the website. That seemed hopeless as well, she realised. Twenty pounds for her brightly coloured rug would be a drop in the bucket to what Dash was to be paid. She couldn't remember the amount exactly.

'I confess I don't sit at mine either,' Dash replied.

She crossed the kitchen. 'D'you know what?' She gave a chuckle, as though she'd been absent minded instead of cupboard bare. 'It's ludicrous, but I don't have any tea or coffee. Or biscuits.'

He seemed not to have heard. Dash sat opposite her on the sofa, with the table between them. His long legs were bent, with knees touching the table--Elena realised she ought to move the sofa out for tall people--and he rested his elbows on his opened knees, hands clasped together. His eyes were cast downward.

'Elena, I wanted to apologise. You see, I meant to say that the email handlers would need advice from your solicitor. But I suppose whatever I said implied that it wasn't feasible. I'm concerned about it, for legal reasons. But it is possible for them to help you.' He looked up at her. 'I felt badly for upsetting you like that.'

'I'm sorry too.'

'Elena, it was entirely--'

'No, Dash. Please. Let me finish. I was at dinner with Willa Purslow yesterday. Your name came up because her mum had asked who else might have a stall at the farmer's market. She said she was glad you're doing well.' Elena realised she was rambling. 'The thing is, I learned about your fiancée. I realised immediately that it is *she* who is represented by the fairy, and my comments about her at the art show...well, I'm not sure that's what I would've said, had I known.'

Dash took a long, laboured breath. Then he said, 'The thing is, you're the first person, *the only person,* who has made an accurate observation of what I was trying to say about her. And what's more remarkable is that you didn't even know about Tricia.'

'You weren't angry?'

'Yes. But not at you.' He stretched both hands out in a frustrated gesture. 'I needed to keep it together that evening. Plus, I don't always talk this much.' He grinned. 'I usually express my feelings by making something, but we were talking, and, well, you know.'

'I do know. A lot of my feelings are in my paintings. It's easier, sometimes.'

They shared another look, reassured by mutual understanding.

Elena ignored the fact that her mouth felt like cotton wool. 'But why were you angry? And at whom?'

'Myself. Not really angry. Frustrated. I've mourned Tricia's death for years now. At times, I thought I'd die from grief. Then, during the installation at the charity art show, I put the fairy in place. I stood back and looked at her. A few nights after the show in Shrewsbury, I had a nightmare about her. But I woke up knowing that I wouldn't dream about her anymore. Somehow, everything had changed.'

Elena's brow wrinkled in confusion.

Dash continued, trying to explain, 'To be honest, it happened in a moment. I went from endless grieving to being *done.* I suddenly felt like I've been wasting my life.' He dropped his head and whispered, 'Sounds dramatic, I know. But the weight just lifted. It's no good, living in the past.'

'And when I "recognised" her as someone you loved?' Elena asked tentatively.

'I just didn't want to talk about her anymore. This must sound really cold--'

'No, Dash, not at all. I think I understand. Everyone says Tricia was lovely, so I'm sure this is what she would've wanted. For you to move on.'

He looked away from the honesty of the moment. A few moments passed and then he smiled. 'I have a big box of builder's tea at home. Not my usual brand, but it must have been on sale or standing in the middle of the aisle or something. It's disgusting, so I suppose I've stopped drinking tea altogether.' He paused and said, 'I do keep running on about nothing.'

She smiled. 'I like to hear you go on about nothing. Even disreputable tea.' She felt herself relax.

It was then that Bryan's text message came.

CHAPTER 27

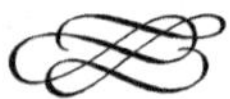

Dash was smiling at her. But as she glanced down at her vibrating phone it read: "URGENT." She picked up the phone and saw that it was a message from Bryan.

"Manager's wife here. In my office. Police?"

Elena wasn't sure how to make sense of the message. 'Nichola?' she said aloud.

'Something wrong?'

'Yes.' Elena stood up and went to put on her shoes and grab her handbag. 'It's Bryan. About my ex-manager, Roman. My guardians. His wife has turned up.'

'What do you mean, turned up?' Dash rose to his feet and followed her towards the cottage door.

Elena called over her shoulder but didn't break pace. 'I must go to Bryan's office.'

She stopped for a moment and sent a reply to Bryan. '*On my way.*'

They both jogged outside. Her hands shook a little as she began to drive. Dash was following in his SUV. Perhaps he'd go as far as Pulverbridge and then continue home. At this point, she was glad there was some sort of understanding between them, but she had no idea if he would insinuate himself into this situation. Whatever it was.

During the drive, Elena felt calm in a surreal sort of way. Her mind turned over the possibilities. Slowing, they made their way through the short distance that constituted the village of Marris Mynd, and then accelerated as they left the village behind. Only five minutes now.

By the time Elena reached Pulverbridge, she felt she had grasped the scenario playing out in Bryan's office. Making contact with Elena would be Nichola's only reason for being in this part of England. Nichola was looking for her. Somehow, via public sales records or stolen financials, Nichola had been able to come as far as Elena's estate agent. Even though Roman Giblin had shown up at Elena's property in Marris Mynd, Nichola must not have quite as much information. If she had done, she surely would've come directly to Elena's cottage at Bytheway.

But what did she want? Maybe she thought Elena had the power to stop the lawsuit against Roman. Mr Deboer had told Elena that Roman had been turned over to the authorities. Elena didn't expect to hear from her solicitor again; he certainly knew that she had no money to pay his expensive fees.

Elena turned into the cramped car park at Bryan's office and took a space by a long black saloon car. There was a driver sitting at the wheel. She opened her vehicle door as Dash pulled into the car park behind her, blocking her in. There was space on the other side of the building, but Bryan's message had ignited in them both a sense of urgency. Elena wondered if Bryan had told Dash about the threatening visit from Roman. It had been Bryan's quick thinking that had allowed her to safely escape the situation. She hoped Bryan was equal to Roman's wife as well.

Dash overtook Elena in the short walk to Bryan's office and

stepped in front of her. He stepped into Bryan's office. She followed.

Nichola sat across from Bryan's desk, mopping her eyes with a tissue. She hopped up and bellowed, 'Oh, darling! I knew you'd come!' She crossed the room, arms wide open.

Dash obviously didn't consider Nichola a danger; he stood aside while Nichola took Elena in an enormous hug.

Elena felt an iciness pass through her chest. She pushed Nichola away. 'What are you doing here?'

'*Eeeelahnaa,*' Nichola whined. 'You were the only person I could turn to; you know you're the closest person I have to family. You're like my daughter, and only you know--'

'That's not true. At best, I was your employee, Nichola. I've paid out well, and now you're going to leave me alone.'

The words sounded familiar in Elena's ears, then she remembered. She was in a private therapy session in hospital. She'd felt woozy from medication.

'If you could speak to Nichola, what would you say?' The therapist looked over his half-lensed reading glasses. His face had been void of emotion and she'd known that nothing she said would shock or upset him.

It felt so self-indulgent to be able to say—or even scream—whatever she wanted, and she had. She'd secretly hoped the therapist would phone Nichola and repeat her words, because she'd wanted Nichola to know how much she'd hurt her. The therapist could make people listen; no one else had ever listened to Elena. Once Elena had started talking, she couldn't seem to stop. The therapist had let her go on and on until her session bell rang and her time was up. She couldn't remember, later, a lot of what she'd said, but the finer points came out of her mouth now.

'You never loved me, Nichola.'

Nichola looked at the two men who were now standing either side of Elena. She was obviously planning a strategy to make the situation go her way. Elena had watched her manipulate men before.

Nichola looked old and haggard. And she, like her husband Roman had been when he came to Shropshire, was a little drunk. 'Elena, you were too young to understand. I wasn't allowed to mother you, you know. Roman wouldn't let me. He--'

'He couldn't have stopped you from loving me. You just didn't. You couldn't. You've never loved anyone but yourself!' Elena's fists hurt from clenching at her sides and her body pitched forward with the force of her yelling.

Nichola's mouth hung open in ugly surprise. 'But I always looked out for you, Elena. I hired people to love you. Nanny Rose, she was only in your life because of me. I was responsible for bringing her in to care for you.'

'And responsible for sacking her three years later for—what was it, Nichola? You accused her of stealing your jewellery. Nanny, who'd never worn anything but a crucifix. You chucked her out of my life as easily as you binned your unwanted clothes.'

Nichola literally stepped back from the words that Elena hurled at her. She reached behind for the wooden office chair and eased herself into it. As Nichola sat down, Bryan rose, as though he refused to sit opposite her at the desk. She propped her elbow on the arm of the chair and pressed her mouth onto the top of her curled fist.

Dash intervened, stepping slightly in front of Elena. 'What do you want, Mrs Giblin?'

Nichola's voice was thin and pathetic, but her eyes were dry. Elena knew that Nichola's gaze was towards the floor so that no one would see the spite that glittered in them.

'You probably don't care, Elena.' Nichola dabbed at an imaginary tear with her fingertip. 'But my poor Roman will be sent to prison because you ran away with no thought for anyone else.

You just disappeared.' She looked up and couldn't hide her contempt. 'You were always ungrateful.'

Just as quickly, Nichola's voice turned to a whine. 'Our assets have been frozen. There's no money. Even our house--the home you grew up in--has been taken away.'

'It sounds as though you're deeply in debt,' Dash said with an even, accusatory tone.

Nichola's head snapped up and she beamed her eyes at him just as some pretty tears were forming. 'Yes, I'm afraid you're right, young man. My husband always spent a lot caring for his clients. I mean, you can see that Elena has money to spare. That left little for us.'

'Monte Carlo enjoyed your custom, Nichola, while I was in hospital.' Elena crossed her arms in front of her, starting to feel emotional now. Her anger had subsided and now she was shaky. Dash seemed to sense her strength wavering, and he put his arm around her and hugged her to his side. She hollowed against him and felt more secure--here in the middle of this bizarre confrontation--than she had in a long time.

Nichola ignored Elena and Dash and turned her efforts to convincing Bryan. 'I have nothing. Roman has...*left* for a while, and I have no family to stand by me. I'm all on my own.'

Dramatics and scheming, Elena thought. *It's really all this woman has ever had.* Manipulation had been her only power for years.

She was leaning over the desk now, cleavage heaving towards Bryan, shrewd tears glistening in her heavily made-up eyes. 'I thought if Elena would come home with me, we could get a place together. Weather the storm, as we have when there were problems before. Remember, darling?' Nichola said with a hollow laugh.

Elena suspected that Nichola had fallen out with her sister. They were always feuding. Or perhaps the sister didn't want to be tainted by the bad press that Roman and Nichola were receiving at the moment. Hortense, Nichola's eldest sister who lived in Germany, would take Nichola in if she could bear to leave London.

Nichola thought she was cunning, Elena realised, because she hadn't yet understood that Roman had completely screwed them both. Seized by a desire to cleave Nichola to the core, Elena spat out the truth. 'Yes. That's because Roman has hidden all the money from you. He's taken all the money from my trust as well. That's why he's spinning that story in the media, acting as though he and I are a couple and my share of the trust fund money is "ours." He's stolen from me.' Elena felt the words stream out of her effortlessly from some deep place. She let the words flow on, 'He's embezzled my entire fortune. A specialist friend of mine supposes he's hidden it and that he'd made investments that neither of us knew about. So, you see, Nichola, when Roman got his hands on the full fortune, he shut you out.'

Nichola's hand went to her throat in surprise.

'He's taken everything from us both, Nichola. Instead of Roman telling you where he's hidden it, he's going to let them turn you out of your luxury home. But I expect he'll be calling you to pay his bail, won't he?'

Nichola slumped in the cheap office chair as the truth came home to roost.

Finding another tactic, Nichola attempted to re-group. 'He betrayed me. After all I've done for him. And after all I've done for you.' The room was silent for some moments. Genuine tears began to fall down Nichola's cheeks. It was the first time Elena had seen her truly cry. 'But you can't help me, can you?' Nichola spat the words.

Elena saw the bitterness in her eyes, and knew that Nichola would soon be on her way now that she had established Elena had no money to give to her.

Elena took a long look at her former guardian, a woman

who'd never tried to behave like a mother towards her. 'Enjoy your trip to Germany,' were Elena's parting words.

She looked up at Dash and he understood. It was time to go.

They walked out of the office. Nichola knew she had been defeated and stood silently and walked out of the office behind them.

Bryan stayed inside, perhaps not wanting to encourage Nichola to turn and begin talking to him again. Elena wondered if perhaps he'd rush to lock the door to his office behind them. She floated in a strange dream-like state to her vehicle and climbed in. Dash closed the door behind her.

Nichola got into the back of her hired car and said something to the driver. She looked at Elena through the window, wearing the expression of a lost child, as the driver backed out onto the road and sped away.

Elena started the ignition and brought down the window. Dash reached out and cupped his fingers alongside the back of her arm. 'All right?'

'Yes.'

'I can drive you home. Bryan can follow and bring me back to Pulverbridge.'

'No, I'm okay. But I need a few minutes first. Then I can take myself off home.'

'Sounds sensible. Give yourself a moment. Do you want to go back inside?'

She suddenly felt light. 'No.'

Struck by the appeal of his ashy green eyes and softly waving dark hair, Elena smiled. 'I want to go over there.' She gestured down the road towards Pulverbridge. 'And see if I can manage a proper taste of that coffee this time.'

Dash grinned broadly. 'Yeah. Okay.'

He got into his vehicle, backed away, and she followed him towards the coffee shop.

CHAPTER 28

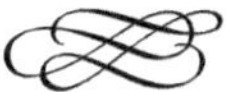

Willa walked around the flower beds lining the farmhouse. She had planted them several years ago with the help of the gardener at Myndcroft Hall. The plants had flourished and became a lovely garden just as Laurence, the old gardener, had promised. The plot design he'd given to Willa had produced successive blooms in every season, in harmonious colours. She had enjoyed her foray into gardening, especially as Laurence allowed her to walk with him at the Hall, helping with plant-related chores and learning the finer points.

She wandered around the garden and contemplated the unusual call she had received this morning. It had been Granny Phoebe who'd phoned.

'Hello, petal. How are the wedding plans?'

'Everything's finished. But I've had all new problems to solve, Gran.'

'Oh?'

'Yes. I met with the vicar's wife, Veronica Hayward, and she had some interesting suggestions for me. She told me I ought to offer myself as a consultant at the tea room where I've been working, and she was spot on. Roni snapped up my offer to design new menus and work out the recipes for her. In fact, she was so quick to settle on the fee that I'm not sure I asked enough.'

'But just as well, since you're gaining experience.'

'That's what I thought.' Willa and Granny usually had similar thoughts when it came to business-related things.

'What else did Mrs Hayward say?'

'She had a compelling idea of running a bed and breakfast out of the Smiths' property. You'll remember the one, Granny, just across the road?'

'Oh, yes. Where was it they went?'

'France.'

'Right. Well, that sounds splendid. And falls in with what I'd wanted to say to you.'

Willa felt a stirring of excitement. Granny's phone calls were few and far between. One never knew what she would say. 'I'm listening, Gran. Should I take notes or something?'

'No, darling. This is an easy suggestion,' Granny said with a chuckle. 'I think you ought to ask Colleen to lunch.'

Willa was stunned. She couldn't have imagined Granny would say *that* in a hundred years of guessing. 'Hmm. Oliver's mum? Really?'

'Don't say "hmm," love. It sounds so unintelligent. Have something at the ready, such as, "Why, that's an interesting suggestion. Tell me more." Far better than grunting, Willa.'

'Why, that's an interesting suggestion, Grandmother. Please, tell me more.'

'I shall, you cheeky girl. Colleen is not the sort to reach out when she ought to, Willa. You'll have to work a bit at making friends. Once you do, she'll be a wonderful support for you.'

'All right. When you said to ask her to lunch...please, Granny, tell me more.'

'Now you're trying my patience,' she said, but with a twinge of amusement in her voice. 'I think you ought to invite her to your home.'

'Oh, Gran. Don't you think she'd much prefer going out, somewhere particularly smart?'

'If I thought that, I would've said. As I've told you before, she comes from a farming family. You're a brilliant cook, Willa. Show Colleen who it is that she's welcoming into her family.'

Willa thought about it a moment, and several impressions she had about Colleen clicked into place. Whilst no one in their right mind would say that Lady Ranson didn't exhibit perfect social graces, it was rather easy to see what Granny meant.

'Who is Colleen's best friend, do you think, Gran?'

'I don't know. But I can see you've grasped the point.'

Willa agreed. 'I still don't entirely understand. You said something about how what you wanted to say fitted in with Mrs Hayward's bed and breakfast idea?'

'Yes, darling. Think of how that idea would play out, should Colleen be in management with you, rather than Oliver.'

She felt Granny was incorrect this time. 'What? Granny, it may surprise you to know that Oliver was quite keen on the idea! Actually, he said he'd helped his mum with related sorts of things at Myndcroft Hall in the past. It's something we want to do together.'

'As you say, poppet.'

It was off-putting when Granny held her peace and refused to comment.

They rang off. Willa went inside. No better time than the present. She poured a glass of water, then picked up her mobile to issue an invitation to Oliver's mother.

Lady Ranson came to lunch at Hilltop Farm the following afternoon. She came bearing a beautiful bouquet and said, 'Laurence was quite proud to send these along with me.'

'Oh, my goodness,' Willa said. The bouquet was too big for any of the vases in the house, so Willa put it in the boot room sink. 'I'll have to sort them later, but I couldn't be more pleased.'

Colleen smiled. 'I'll let him know.'

'We're in here, if you'd like to come through.'

Willa came into the dining room and Colleen followed. The table was set with a light pink cloth, Lisa's floral china that she'd left behind at the farmhouse, and crystal drinking glasses. A simple arrangement of pink and white tulips stood in a purple glass vase at the centre of the table.

They sat down and were about the business of unfolding their dining napkins when Colleen said, 'Oh, Willa, this is all very lovely. You know, I was trying to remember when I was last here, in the house. Sadly, it was the day your father was discovered. Perhaps I shouldn't have mentioned it.'

Willa assured her that the memory hadn't stung. 'Actually, my first thought was, "My mother didn't entertain very often."' They laughed.

'But instead, she's always done a marvellous job bringing the entire village and surrounding area together for the annual arts festival,' Colleen remarked.

'And you've done a fabulous job taking over the reins after she moved to Ludlow.'

'Your mother gave me very good instructions about how to carry everything off, you know. But things are changing just enough that I think this year will represent a learning curve for me.'

'Would it help if I pledged myself to be your volunteer?' Willa asked.

'I would so appreciate it, Willa. I've learned in the past that things are easily solved when you can share ideas; but I've also learned that not every idea should be up for discussion. There seems to be a point where a little leadership of one person saying, "This is the direction we need to go" can give people a focus.'

'Yes, I see what you mean.'

And I see what Granny meant too, thought Willa. Although Oliver was willing to help, Colleen may be more passionate about the day-to-day running of the B&B with her. She sensed that she and Colleen would feed off one another's enthusiasm. She would mention Veronica's suggestion before their lunch was through and note Colleen's response.

Elena had finally tasted the delicious coffee at Dash's beloved shop in Pulverbridge, and they'd been chatty and charged with energy after the confrontation with Nichola. Now the conversation was becoming a bit more serious.

'Obviously I had no idea what you were going through, and I know of a way I can help,' Dash told Elena. She began to protest, and he laid a finger across her lips. 'Don't,' he said, and she began to giggle. 'Just hear me out. I think I ought to load up some images of the new work you've done—whatever you're willing to part with, that is, or whatever you chose to make prints of—and create an online store on your website. Then you'll truly be in business.'

'You can do that? Oh, Dash, that would be wonderful. I don't know how to ship anything.'

'I do. There's a parcel shop in Church Stretton that will box up your artwork and send it on to your customer, anywhere in the world, insured and fully tracked. It's well worth the price. I found that buying the packaging supplies was more expensive out of pocket, and they do a better job.'

'What a relief. I'm not really certain what the market for my art is right now. But for a long time, I've wanted to have some options. I want to do more sculptures and ceramics. And instead of only offering paintings, I'd like to be able to have some less expensive options: prints, greeting cards, and so forth.

Particularly for organisations that would like to use those types of items for fundraising.' Elena's cheeks coloured and she grew quiet.

'I know about the problem with the auction.'

'It's beyond embarrassment. It's a broken promise. The hospital won't get the proceeds as was my intention. And I've missed having your beautiful tree in my cottage.'

'I've spoken with the woman handling the charity auctions for the hospital. She's simply going to re-auction the piece at an upcoming event in Leicester. It's worked out a treat. I was invited to exhibit again; the feeling was it helps people get more out of the evening, and perhaps be more inclined to bid on the art.'

'Oh, what a relief. That's simply a dream turnaround of the whole mess, isn't it?'

Dash took her hand. 'Not to mention, I'm going to make you another piece, and it will be free of charge.'

'It's too generous, Dash, especially when I owe you money,' Elena said. But as she gazed into his eyes, she read his feelings. 'Thank you,' she said with a laugh.

CHAPTER 29

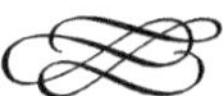

'That's lovely, Sarah.' Elena finished taking pictures of her young neighbour. She picked up her sketchbook and pencil and, with deft strokes, she captured Sarah's form, sitting beneath a cherry tree, a book open in her lap. Elena had taken other pictures of Sarah walking through the alley of cherry trees wearing a white smocked dress with blue forget-me-nots embroidered on the collar.

Elena worked for a few minutes. With her older sister's encouragement, Sarah was a perfect artist's model, both quiet and compliant. After she'd done a number of sketches and realised that little Sarah's eyes had begun to sneak glances this way and that, she felt she had enough reference material.

'Sarah, you did so well! Thank you.' She turned to Charlotte, 'And you were very helpful. I appreciate your helping me, and for both of you being as quiet as little mice while I worked.'

Sarah was on her feet, hands cradling her book. Both girls smiled at Elena's compliments but didn't say a word.

'How about coming into my cottage for a treat before you go home? Your mum said she wouldn't mind.'

Sarah pranced around the lawn with delight, singing something to herself. Elena turned to Charlotte and said, 'I don't think I've ever known a child who sings more often than Sarah.'

'I know. Mum is concerned about it.'

'How so?'

'Sarah often doesn't want to say anything. It seems like she can't gather her thoughts or something. So sometimes she'll sing instead of talking at all.'

'Curious, isn't it?'

'Very. Some experts looked at her, and couldn't really find any reason for it.'

Sarah was waiting for them at the cottage door, hopping like a bunny rabbit, which pushed some lyrics out louder than the rest. Elena whispered to Charlotte, 'Happy little bunny, though.'

Charlotte smiled. 'That she is.'

Elena put her phone and sketches down on the sofa table. As she turned around, Charlotte was already in the kitchen, filling the kettle and expertly placing it on the hob. Elena was pleased; her teenage friend was making herself useful and feeling at home, and that was a lovely thing. She hadn't had any visitors to a space of her own before moving here. Living out of suitcases, making appearances, and working out of hired spaces had taken their toll, and she had survived in the way that best suited her, through her behaviour and actions. Elena thought that everyone had an individual way of making sense of the world. Perhaps that was behind little Sarah's insistence on singing as her main form of communication.

Elena opened a cupboard for the plates and mugs, but allowed Charlotte to carry on making the tea without interruption. 'This is the first time I've ever baked anything in my life,' Elena said, opening a tin. She'd filled the small pantry when she first moved in, and so had the ingredients on hand to try a recipe for simple jammy biscuits she'd found online. She'd also used some of the money in her handbag for an economical but delicious box of Yorkshire tea from Sally's shop.

'Really?' Charlotte asked, amazed. Elena guessed that Charlotte's mum, Bess, had taught her daughter all sorts of helpful domestic skills.

They sat down together, properly, at the kitchen table.

'These are good,' Charlotte said of the biscuits.

Elena agreed with her and felt a ridiculous sense of pride at having made the recipe.

Charlotte chatted about getting an email from Phoebe.

'I visited her house with Willa,' Elena confessed. 'But Phoebe wasn't there for very long.'

Elena noticed a look of annoyance cross Charlotte's face. Ludlow and Phoebe were probably a destination that Charlotte longed for, and here was Elena, just casually dropping by Phoebe's family home.

'She may as well live in China.'

It wasn't like Charlotte to be sulky, and Elena was unsure what to say. 'Yes, it can seem like that sometimes. Was her email interesting?'

Charlotte immediately brightened. 'She apologised that she didn't make it back to Marris Mynd for Easter. We were going to sit together in church and then go to Hilltop Farm. Willa was making a big lunch or something.'

Elena knew the pang of feeling like an outsider. 'I was on my own for Easter too.'

Charlotte pulled a shocked face at this. Apparently, she hadn't considered that a grown-up could feel friendless as well. Surprisingly, her eyes suddenly filled. 'I'm sorry.'

Elena reached over and laid a hand on her shoulder. 'Oh, Charlotte. Don't feel badly. It wasn't your fault. I only wanted you to know that everyone feels lonely sometimes, and there are seasons in your life when you may not have a best friend.'

'What do you do? I mean, how do you get through it?' Charlotte looked overwhelmed, and Elena struggled for a moment to say the right thing. She remembered how difficult it was to be fifteen.

'I think it's best to be grateful for what you have. The people that you do know. No matter how little you have, and even if you don't have friends to share with. Remember that your misery is temporary,' Elena felt she was talking to herself as much as Charlotte. 'Think happy thoughts. And, you must do things that make you happy, too. That's why I paint, and why Sarah sings, isn't it, Sarah?' Elena laughed and added, 'That was quite the speech. I hope you'll remember it!'

Charlotte giggled, and Sarah did too.

The girls left a few minutes later, by the time appointed by Bess for them to be home. Clearing the dishes, Elena's thoughts went back to yesterday.

She and Dash had sat at his usual table at the coffee shop. They'd only had a few minutes before Dash needed to leave for an appointment. He'd seemed quite different in his demeanour towards her; she wasn't sure how much of that was their friendly banter at her cottage before Bryan contacted her, or how much it came down to Dash taking Elena's side in the emotionally-charged scene with Nichola. Whatever the explanation, he seemed more accessible.

'How is it?' Dash had waited for Elena's verdict on the coffee.

'Delicious. The third time's a charm.'

Dash had smiled, without looking away, as had been his habit in their previous meetings.

'I feel rather embarrassed that you and Bryan witnessed that awful row with Nichola. Please remember it's been years in the making. She and her husband controlled my life. I've been waiting a long time to say some of those things.'

'I don't think less of you for it. I think more of you.'

Elena had been staggered by his reply. 'What? I'm not sure I understand what you mean. We were two crying, shouting females. It was such a mess.' This time, it was she who'd pulled her eyes away from his.

'Despite the tears, I was proud of you. It was obvious you needed to draw a line in the sand. And anyone could tell that she and her husband are fairly formidable people, used to getting their way.'

'Thank you. It means a lot that you understood. I think Bryan does too. He's had the pleasure of meeting both of the Giblins now.'

'He does. He told me about meeting Roman. Bryan thought he was a bit scary.'

'He is.'

'But now look at you.' She and Dash had stared at each other a long moment after he'd said that.

Elena wasn't sure what he'd been thinking, but her own thoughts were pretty basic. Dash was positively gorgeous, inside and out. No wonder she couldn't be more in love with him.

They'd talked on and on about art and the places they had travelled. After loaded glances from the coffee bar staff, they realised they'd been sitting there chatting for hours.

'Now that I know the true state of things, we're stopping by the grocery before you go off home.'

'What do you need? Are you much of a cook?' Elena asked.

'Not for me. For you.' Dash stopped outside the coffee shop door. 'And there will be no arguments. I've had a very good month, not to mention you'd do the same for me.'

She smiled, looking forward to the trip to the grocery, not because of the food he would purchase for her, but because they got to spend more time together, wandering the shop aisles, laughing, talking, and learning more about one another.

CHAPTER 30

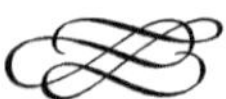

It had been eight hours since she'd heard from Dash. It felt like eight years. She missed him, but she wasn't concerned. Elena knew now that his feelings matched hers; every time she thought of him, her heart felt full.

A Mozart concerto accompanied her brush strokes. The portrait of Sarah sitting under the tree was, as yet, only shapes and values of an undeveloped background laid in, with her hair, face, and neck emerging little by little. Getting the little girl's lucid skin tone just exactly right would be a little challenging, and she began mixing the hue of Sarah's peachy-pink cheek colour on her palette.

Elena had brought her mobile into the studio for the first time since she'd been living and working here. It was a necessity now. She was rewarded for keeping it close when Dash rang her at noon.

'Have you eaten lunch yet?'

'Is it lunchtime?'

He laughed. 'You're painting, then?'

'Yes. It's coming together so beautifully. Sarah may already be one of my favourite models ever.'

'I'm sorry I've been on radio silence.'

'No worries,' Elena said, daubing her brush mindlessly on a kitchen towel. 'I knew you'd call when you caught up with whatever it is.'

'Exactly right. And now I want to have lunch with you and show you something.'

'Show me what?'

'Where I live. Who I live with.'

'You live with someone?'

'Yes.'

They'd agreed to meet at the pub in Marris Mynd for lunch. He'd gotten there first, as usual. And he'd kissed her before walking into the restaurant. They ate a perfect order of fish and chips. He said, 'Shall I drive us from here? I don't know why I didn't come to pick you up at your place.'

'Because you were excited and didn't think of it.'

'Yes, you're exactly right.'

The pub car park was generous, and so she left her vehicle and got into his and he drove toward Pulverbridge. He turned on the road that she already knew he lived on. Then he turned left again, and began driving down a long lane. There were woods on either side.

'It's quite odd, really.'

'What?' she asked him. She'd just been thinking of him kissing her.

'You'll see.'

When they arrived, she did see.

'Dash, that's just *strange.*'

They got out of the vehicle and walked towards the door of a cottage that looked nearly like a perfect copy of Elena's own cottage.

'There's a simple explanation,' he said, opening the door for her.

His home was a masculine version of her own. It smelled

deliciously of a small pine tree planted in a terracotta pot by a wood burner.

'It's so cosy,' Elena said. 'I love your pieces here.'

A bronze of an eagle graced a small table by the door, and another bird, its wings spread in flight, hung on the wall. As she had done, Dash had set up a wooden table and chairs in the kitchen, but it lacked a homey range like hers. He also had a similar arrangement by the fire, but instead of a sofa and two chairs, he had two large sofas in worn dark leather, facing one another. The windows were bare of curtains, there were no soft rugs on the floor. The lack of feminine touches signaled to Elena that Dash's fiancé probably hadn't lived here before she passed away.

'I'll go get my flatmate.' Dash walked towards the bedroom door and opened it. A black Labrador came charging out, wagging his entire body, greeting her with a friendly whine. He had paws that were too big, signifying that he was still a pup.

'Stay down, Coal,' Dash reminded him.

'Oh, aren't you sweet?' Elena was instantly down on the floor with the dog so that he wouldn't be scolded for jumping up. He smiled and rolled onto his back, offering up his soft tummy for a rub. His friendliness made Elena laugh and Dash joined them on the floor, resting his back on one of the sofas. In a moment, Coal jumped up, surging with puppy energy, and galloped off to the kitchen. Elena waited, smiling. Then Coal came trotting back again, proudly carrying a toy duck in his mouth. This he dropped on Elena's lap.

'You know you're only allowed to fetch outside.'

Coal responded with a whine and threw himself down on his belly, submissively laying his chin on his front paws.

'He is so adorable!' Elena said, picking up the duck and offering it to him. Coal growled in play and tugged on it, too hard, pulling Elena up off her seat. She smiled and Dash intervened again, taking over the pulling match with the dog.

'He really needs a long walk. Do you mind?'

'I'd love to,' she said, getting to her feet and putting on her coat.

'You got a new one.'

'You noticed,' Elena said, pulling her hair from the collar. She'd sold the landscape painting, the first work she'd done in Marris Mynd. 'I celebrated and did some shopping with Willa in Church Stretton. I've been warm and dry ever since. It's a good thing.'

'It is. They have some nice places to eat there. Would you like to go on Saturday night?'

'Yes. If they're terribly smart, you'll see me in the same dress I wore to the auction. It's the only dressy thing I have.'

'The place I was thinking of is more casual, but the food is excellent. Do you like Italian?'

'I love it. Especially ravioli.'

'They've got it and it's a favourite.'

'You'll have to stop talking or we'll need to go this evening.'

They walked along a wide path through a thin wood. At the end of the track, there was a clearing and a pond. Coal raced back and forth along the water's edge, his ears flying out to the sides. He grunted as he stretched his legs forward each pace, loving the sheer exuberance of speed. Dash threw the duck and Coal masterfully retrieved it, and brought it back.

'He loves to swim, but I don't want him to drench you,' Dash said. 'He tends to come too close and then shakes, leaving you wetter than he was when he came out of the pond.'

As they walked back towards Dash's cottage, Coal ran ahead and then back to them.

'You said there was a simple explanation of why our cottages look alike.'

Dash reached out for her hand. 'Do you like holding hands?'

'I don't know.'

Dash laughed. 'How can you not know?'

'I've never had a boyfriend, and it's been a long time since Nanny held my hand.'

Dash pulled on her hand to stop her walking forward. 'Would you consider letting me have the title?'

Elena tipped her face up towards him. 'Don't boyfriends need an audition?'

He kissed her.

'You've got the job.' They laughed and he wrapped her in his arms. When they had been kissing so long that the damp cold of the grass began coming up through her trainers, they reluctantly stopped and walked back to the cottage. Elena discovered that she did, indeed, like holding hands.

Once they were warming themselves in front of the woodstove, Dash answered her question. 'Our cottages were built by the same family. Their name was Teece, and you can see their gravestones in several of the village plots in the area.'

'How did you come to know that?'

'I bought my cottage from one of the family. He told me that the other pair at Bytheway belonged to them once, and also a big farm outside of Church Stretton.'

'What did the family do?'

'They farmed and kept cows. You know there's a shed between your house and the Seabury's land? That was a piggery at one time.'

'It seems that's the only building at Bytheway that the Smiths didn't refurbish.'

'No need, really. They used it for storage.'

Talking about the farmers who'd occupied their cottages led to a discussion about Dash's own family. Elena learned that his parents had divorced, and his brother had gone

to live in New York for his work at a large social media corporation.

'I was close to my dad, but we've grown apart now. He

remarried, you see, and she's from Cornwall. They've moved down there and had a baby. I don't really fit into his new life.'

'But he's happy?'

'Yes. So, I'm happy for him.'

They talked about lots of things. Schools they'd been to, places they'd visited, and friends that had come and gone or stayed. Just after midnight, Elena finally ended their lunch date. In the darkness of her car, she smiled, reflecting on various things they'd said.

She couldn't believe her luck. And her depth of happiness.

THE MORNING BROUGHT a sky bruised with rain clouds. Elena felt restless and was eating her toast by the fire, a warmth courtesy of the faux logs Dash had bought her during their shopping spree at the grocery in Pulverbridge. Her mobile rang and she smiled as she picked it up, all dark moods immediately taking flight.

'HELLO, YOU!' she said, still chewing her breakfast.

There was a pause at the other end of the phone. 'Miss Dalca?'

She didn't answer, fearful that it may have something to do with Roman or Nichola.

'I'm sorry to phone out of the blue. This is Bill Barker, Bryan's father at the estate agents'. I'm afraid we've somehow never met in person, but Bryan said you wouldn't mind my ringing you.'

Relief made her buoyant. 'Oh, Mr Barker. How lovely to finally speak with you. Thank you again for everything you've done for me.'

'My pleasure, Miss Dalca. I'll come right to the point, as we may want to go through the whole process all over again. You see, I've had a generous offer for your property, though of course it isn't currently on offer. I understand you're acquainted with Lady Ranson?'

'Not directly, but I know who she is,' Elena replied.

'Well, she's been in contact, you see. She'd like to make Bytheway the most...*remarkable* wedding gift to her son and his fiancé, Willa Purslow. Would that be something you'd be open to discussing, Miss Dalca?'

She'd never realised how much the property felt like a millstone. Just last week, she'd learned that the local chaps wanted over 500 pounds to mow the thickly grown spring lawn.

'Yes, Mr Barker. I'd be delighted to hear what Lady Ranson has in mind.'

'I'm so pleased to hear it. I think you'll find she has been quite sensitive to the increasing value of property in the area, and she's even willing to separate any buildings you're currently using to house business ventures from the sale of the main house.'

Elena blushed as she recalled a hint from Dash about their making a home together. An outsider may have thought they were moving a bit too quickly, but Elena wanted nothing more than to be close to him.

'Would it suit your schedule to come to the office to learn more? I can share all of the details on paper.'

'Certainly. Just let me know a time that is convenient for you, Mr Barker and I will be there!'

EPILOGUE

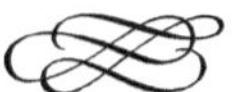

The long-awaited weekend in June had finally arrived, and the wedding was going perfectly to plan. Elena sat next to Dash and Charlotte in the second row. Charlotte had wanted to be up close and to sit with Elena instead of her own family.

Willa looked positively radiant, and Oliver thrilled with his choice. Behind the bride stood her sister, Mollie, looking less a goat farmer and more like her part-time role as a fashion model in her blush pink gown. Next to her was Willa's youngest sister, Phoebe, who was having a difficult time keeping her tears at bay. Phoebe gripped the flowers in her hands, and her shoulders shook periodically from her weeping. Elena imagined that it was their polar opposite natures that caused her and Charlotte to be friends. But, although Phoebe was often neglectful at keeping in touch, Elena thought she had been very sweet the moment she'd seen Charlotte. Phoebe had run up to her--letting everyone present see her in her bridesmaid gown--to give Charlotte a hug.

Elena looked at her young friend. Charlotte's eyes were misty, probably less because Willa was getting married and more because Charlotte felt Phoebe's misery of emotion. That's what friendship was like, Elena thought. And in that sense, she was glad that Dash and Bryan had both stood by her when she'd confronted Roman and Nichola. It had been mortifying, but she'd also felt their strength, support, and even more, their acceptance. They were her closest friends. Willa and her family, Veronica and Stephen Hayward, the Seaburys, and Sally and Tom Andrews—they were all gems. Elena was grateful.

Dash shifted in his seat and slipped his arm around her shoulders. She looked up at him, and he smiled at her and gave her shoulders a squeeze. Then she felt him extend his hand and give Charlotte a friendly pat on the shoulder. Elena could see the girl blush and drop her chin, a huge grin on her face.

Later, after the reception dinner had finished, Elena went to sit by Willa's mother. 'It's all happened so fast,' Lisa said. 'Only a couple of months ago, I met you and told you about Dash's sad history. Now look at the pair of you!'

'Yes, it's all been so lovely. I'm so glad that I left London and came to Marris Mynd. It's really hard to remember how wretched my life was before.'

'There were times when we could all see how miserable Dash was as well, but there was nothing for it but time. And now you'll have to fill me in on this property venture! Willa was hardly making sense on the phone, and I haven't had a chance to interrogate her.'

Sam returned with coffee for him and his wife. 'Oh, good,' he said. 'We're about to get the details, are we?'

Elena said, 'It's quite simple, really. Oliver bought my property for Willa's wedding present. And she and Colleen are thrilled about their plans to reinstate it as a bed and breakfast.'

Sam said, 'That's amazing.'

'But on the other hand, not at all surprising,' Lisa added.

'No, it isn't,' Sam agreed. 'I remember the first time I came to dinner at Hilltop Farm. Willa was in her element, entertaining us all, and her cooking was absolutely smashing. All her skills will come into play with this new venture. Don't you think so, sweetheart?'

'Oh, yes. And Colleen's too. She has a flair for marketing, managing people, and balancing books. They really complement each other.'

'And so do she and Oliver,' Elena said, as the bride and groom approached their wedding cake to cut it. Sam, Lisa, and Elena left their chairs to walk closer to the couple.

'Don't you dare,' Willa warned Oliver, who moved the cake precariously close, but didn't smear her cheek with it. They fed each other wedding cake and kissed for the cameras.

Suddenly, little Sarah ran forward and pointed at Willa. 'Pwincess!' she exclaimed.

A collective gasp of surprise emanated from the crowd. Willa immediately leant down. 'Sarah! You spoke, in front of all of these people!'

Sarah laid her hand on Willa's dress. 'Princess!' she said, her pronunciation already improved. Bess was there in a moment with tears in her eyes, hugging her daughter.

A WEEK LATER, Elena drove into Dash's driveway. She'd brought with her a few items for lunch that she'd purchased at the coffeeshop in Pulverbridge. Coal bounded up to meet her.

'Hello, manky boy, you smell as though you've been swimming in something a bit slimy.'

Coal bounced ahead of her towards the cottage. Elena put the food away and went in search of her boyfriend.

Dash was up on a scaffold with his friend, Kyle, as they placed a roof beam.

Waiting until the precarious bit was over, Elena then called up to him. 'It's really coming along, isn't it?'

Dash turned and smiled as Kyle waved a hello, then set about double-checking the beam's position.

'Hey, beautiful. You'll have a studio before you know it.' Dash came down from his perch and wiped perspiration off his forehead with his sleeve.

'I've brought us lunch, but I didn't know Kyle was here this morning.'

'No worries, he'll be going in a minute. He's got other things on this afternoon.'

He kissed her.

'You and your dog smell a bit earthy. But I love you.'

'Prove it and feed me.'

They laughed and walked arm in arm towards Dash's cottage--soon to be Elena's home as well.

www.ingramcontent.com/pod-product-compliance
Lightning Source LLC
LaVergne TN
LVHW010652110826
845149LV00014B/3053
* 9 7 8 0 9 9 0 6 9 9 5 4 5 *